Marcus Douglas Presents

Dimension of the Soul

By Marcus Douglas

I0563288

Overture 1 – Soul's Dimensions

Is your soul just a part of you, or is it the essence of who you truly are? Some believe it's the deepest part of our being, while others see it as one with the spirit. But what if your soul is more complex than we often assume? Your soul is not a single entity but rather a dynamic combination of three key elements: your mind, your emotions, and your will.

Your mind is the command center of your soul, constantly analyzing, calculating, and processing the world around you. Every decision you make is filtered through its vast amount of knowledge. If you were to hit the lottery, what you do with the money would be based on the information your mind has gathered thus far. The mind plays a significant role in the decision-making process, but that role depends on the individual.

Your emotions are the feeler. Sympathy, empathy, compassion, love, hurt—all filter through your emotions. Emotions are powerful forces that can inspire acts of kindness or drive people to destruction. Love, anger, and fear have shaped history, influencing both the greatest heroes and the most infamous villains. If we use the same lottery example as before, your emotions could play a big part in how that money is spent, but once again, that depends on the individual.

Finally, there is your will, the force that determines whether you persevere or surrender. It is the engine behind ambition, resilience, and determination. For a lack of better words, it is a striving to do or not do, and that could be good or bad. Once again, using the same hypothetical scenario, if you won the lottery, your will would be paying off debt or investing.

How do you personally view your soul?

Marcus Douglas

Chapter 1 – Miles on his Soul

November 5th, 2024

The White House stood tall and proud, surrounded by its meticulously maintained, lush, green lawn. The perfect backdrop for the monumental events that were about to unfold, the scene would captivate the entire nation. Secret Service agents were on high alert, constantly scanning the grounds for potential threats.

A gentle breeze rustled through the air, adding to the sense of anticipation and excitement. The atmosphere was charged with a kinetic energy as the crowd erupted into cheers and applause. People from all over had gathered here today, drawn by the chance to witness history in the making.

The roar of the crowd was overwhelming and infectious, as if a great explosion had just occurred. The excitement was contagious, lingering even after the event that took place only five minutes ago. For the first time, the spectators' cheers traveled faster than the news of what had happened.

The Speaker of the House, Mathew Holeman, was trying to speak over the ruckus assembly. He said, "Wow, okay!"

Mathew was amazed at how loud the crowd was, then proceeded to say with genuine happiness, "This man needs no introduction; he is a leader to others, and he is also a fighter, a man not afraid to lift his sleeves. He is my friend. I present to you our 47th President of the United States, President Kirklin F. Adams and Vice President Justin Porter!"

A lot of family and friends were in attendance to celebrate the triumph of this historical event.

Never had a candidate come so out of nowhere to become the President of the United States.

Stanely and Helana Adams, the President-elect's father and mother, had a huge hand in molding Adams' life. They were one of the many reasons he was in his current position. Several key Republican and Democratic officials were in attendance in support, but the surprise guest was senator Bryan W. Carter. Carter had voted for Adams's Democratic adversary, Carl Simmons, but that was only to keep up with appearances. Carter had low-key put all his faith, finances, and time in Adams. He had also, for all parties, kept his distance. If it wasn't for Carter being in the back pulling the strings, Adams would have not even been heard of, let alone becoming President.

The President-elect came to the podium. A mighty standing ovation with thunderous applause greeted him. He paused to take in all the unwavering excitement.

Trying to calm the crowd, he said, "Thank you, thank you, I am so honored!

"As I stand before you, my fellow Americans, on this momentous day that I have dreamed of for over ten years, elation courses through my veins. When I was a child, my father told me, 'The weight of leadership is heavy, son, but bear it with pride.' And today, I stand before you ready to carry that burden. The weight of this honor is not lost on me – to be chosen by you to hold the great office, to serve as a leader among leaders. I follow in the footsteps of a long line of courageous men who have sacrificed everything for the privilege of being called President. Seeing my name listed alongside these iconic figures is a blessing beyond measure, one that I will cherish and honor with every fiber of my being. This responsibility is not one I will take lightly or squander; it is a sacred trust that I am determined to uphold with all my heart and soul. With your support and guidance, together, we will build a brighter future for our nation. Thank you, from the bottom of my heart."

Adams looked around at the shouting crowd as he continued, "I am indebted to many for their unwavering love and support, to God above, to my beloved wife, Sharron Adams, and my dedicated parents, Mr. and Mrs. Stanely Adams. But above all, I owe a debt of gratitude to the American people. Your tireless efforts in the election, your resilience in our darkest moments – these are what make you truly remarkable. You have shown unbreakable determination when there seemed to be no reason to carry on.

"Uhh… Uhh… You had no reason to withstand the tide."

Adams's voice quivered as he spoke, his words catching in his throat. A sheen of moisture gathered in his brown eyes, and soon, tears began to trickle down his cheeks, leaving glistening trails in their wake.

Adams put his scripted speech to the side and turned towards the audience, understanding that speaking from the heart would resonate more deeply. His words drifted out into the crowd, illuminated by the stage lights and carried away on a gentle breeze in the Washington air.

As the tears sprinkled lightly across his face, Adams regained his composure as he let out a very weak but solemn, "Can I be real with you all?"

The crowd was filled with a sense of awe and shock as they witnessed Adams' unscripted gesture. In a bold move, the President-elect had disregarded his prepared speech and opted to speak candidly. His words were raw and transparent, exposing his true emotions. But while all eyes were fixed on the President-elect pouring his heart out, Senator Carter stood off stage with his back towards Adams. Standing right by a floor speaker, he seemed detached from the powerful moment unfolding before them.

Carter silently followed Adams's words, as if the senator were a ventriloquist or a puppet master, subtly directing the President-elect's gestures and mimicking his tears and expression.

"You, you have sacrificed so much, and it's your efforts that have gotten us to this point. So, thank you, thank you for your vigilance, thank you for your steadfastness. Every burden, loss, misery, trial, and tribulation has gotten us to this point. But although we praise you for your perseverance, now, right now, the work has begun. If you supported me through this journey, then you know what we have to do. We have to secure a better future, and to get it, we have to fight for it," said Adams.

———

While the nation celebrated its new leader, in the shadows, another kind of history was being made, one far more sinister. In a basement of Dapper Industries – an infamous steel mill plant – an illicit transaction of the highest caliber was taking place. It marked the beginning of a new era of terror. A large number of top-of-the-line explosives were being exchanged.

"Hey, we doing this or what?" asked Tank aggressively as he looked at the five buyers.

The different gentlemen who, for the sake of obscurity, went by one letter in the alphabet – J, K, T, G, and P – gave an array of nods to proceed.

{The President-elect continued his speech: "And to America's enemies, we know your heart, you all unify happily at our destruction and demise."}

Tank looked in the back of the building and yelled out, "Stacks, you're up!"

A compound specialist hobbled up to the five gentlemen, chemical burns marring the right side of his face.

His whole being looked like he had a lot of miles on his soul. The man's right side had the outer workings of a raisin. He also walked with a slight limp.

"Good afternoon, gentlemen. This device is truly a work of the highest caliber of devastation," said Stacks ominously.

He limped his deformed body toward a section of the building covered with a curtain. He removed it as the gentlemen stepped forward. The room, composed of new and old technology, had a state-of-the-art fireproof glass wall.

They looked at three old, beat down rooms. From their vantage point, they saw where the rooms converged, allowing them to see the effect of the bomb in each of the chambers. Several rats occupied each room, to show the magnitude of damage the bomb had on live flesh.

{The President-elect continued, "Look as they gather their weapons of mass destruction, seeking to destroy our economy, our way of life – but most importantly, our peace."}

Stacks continued, "Gentlemen, allow me to demonstrate my new explosive, an invisible explosive gas, or IXG.

"The switch is a remote the starts a series of countdowns when this button is smashed," he said as he brought up the remote and mashed the button. "If you look into the middle room on the floor, there is a quiet device, no bigger than a beach ball. The dimensions are twelve by eight; the weight is 88.4 pounds. The remote has the detonation range of six point four kilometers or four miles."

Stacks cast his gaze in the room with the device, and so did the rest of the potential buyers.

"So, as you can see, the device is putting out an odorless gas. In a building like this, with just three rooms, this takes about four minutes. With a building with a lot of rooms to the max of its power, it will take about an hour," said Stacks.

They noticed the rats running, squeaking and squirming in absolute pain. Their screeches faded into nothing.

P asked, "Is this chemical?"

{The President cried out, "God, why can't they see; why are they so blind to the destruction they are causing? Why can't they see the mayhem that will be inflicted on us?"}

Tank bypassed the question, giving out special glasses to the potential buyers. As they all looked through the lenses, they saw a remarkable blue flame that was otherwise invisible to the naked eye. They noticed the damage this device could do. But that wasn't even the half of it. The sprinklers went off, dousing the flames.

The room erupted angrily, and the fire burned more furiously. If the fire had a personality, it would be rage.

The blue flames burned with such intensity that the special glasses flared brightly. The onlookers had to pull them off.

{Adams bellowed out, "Everything pure that we freely give to try and stop this madness, it just makes things worse.}

Stacks smiled confidently, with an almost disgusting pride. "Therein lies my greatest creation. A compound known as ZXH-56 that enhances the abilities of the gas when exposed to water.

"Anything done to try and stop it will just enrage it times twenty. It is truly a thing of beauty," he said, in awe of his work.

Tank gave a slick smile. "Now, I know the asking price was originally $400,000, but seeing the damage the devices could do, my price is now $600,000."

"I knew this was going to happen!" T blurted as he stormed off furiously but eventually came back to the negotiations.

The other buyers murmured to each other.

"Where do we need to transfer the money to?"

Tank said excitedly, "I knew you all would see it my way. My account number is on the back of the first remote in your box. When you successfully pay the amount, it will activate the devices."

All the buyers paid the money and now had their devices. They could wreak havoc on whom they deemed worthy. What they had were ticking time bombs.

{The President-elect confidently stated, "But we have Dimensions."}

Out of nowhere, an older white gentleman entered the abandoned building. It was almost comical, like he'd made a wrong turn and accidentally stumbled down the wrong street. This was an illegal deal of the highest caliber he'd walked into, with some of the most dangerous and sadistic men walking God's green earth.

"Hello, guys, my name is Joseph Hayes. I'm with the FBI, and you all are under arrest."

Tank pulled his gun out and blurted, "Bro, where'd you come from, and how did you find this building?"

Joseph calmly said, "Put the gun down, Tank, or should I call you Jahiem Barr?"

Everyone thought it was a joke, even Tank, until Joseph said his legal name.

Joseph had his hands in his pockets like, in the back of his mind, he knew he was safe.

Tank pointed his gun at Joseph, pulled the trigger, and it clicked.

Joseph emptied Tank's bullets out of his pocket and said very calmly, "Yeah, I took these out of your gun at 5:31 p.m."

"Oh no," Stacks screamed. "It's Dimensions!"

He immediately dropped to his knees with his hands behind his head. Stacks had dealt with killers, arms dealers, and mob bosses. But Dimensions? That was a whole different nightmare.

{President Adams said, "They help with the balance of life. They give a significant advantage to the good side. Dimensions are pro-stability; they are for the very foundation of peace, where our hope is built."}

Tank put his gun on the floor and was amazed that the federal agent disarmed him without even pulling his own weapon. Tank followed Stacks' lead – nothing scared Stacks, but Dimensions had him instantly spooked. Tank surrendered without knowing the full severity of how the man got in and how he knew.

The buyers all fled but were caught where they thought they would escape with ultimate precision. One by one, they were thrown in the back of the wagon.

Back at the White House, the President-elect was finishing his speech. Senator Carter was still mouthing Adams' speech like he wrote it.

"We are at the conclusion of this part of our journey. But, tomorrow, my loved ones, new tasks await us, new trails to face, new crosses to bear, and problems to conquer. And they will not be easy to overcome, but we must Because everything is up to us. Our loved ones depend on us; our present depends on us and, most importantly, our future. Thank you again, and I love you all."

The President-elect waved as he walked off the stage.

Overture 2 – The Soul vs the Spirit

Have you ever wondered about the difference between the soul and the spirit? The Bible tells us that they are not the same, but what truly separates them? The Bible says in Hebrews 4:12, "For the word of God is alive and active. Sharper than any double-edged sword, it penetrates even to dividing soul and spirit, joints and marrow; it judges the thoughts and attitudes of the heart."

This scripture highlights four key elements: the Word of God, the soul, the spirit, and the heart. While each plays a vital role in our faith, today, I want to focus on the relationship between the soul and the spirit—two aspects of our being that are often misunderstood. The spirit is the eternal part of our being. When our flesh gets old and passes away, our mind and heart start to wither and return to the dirt where it was created. But our spirit will still be alive. The spirit is our connection to God. Romans 8:16 says, "The Spirit himself testifies with our spirit that we are God's children." Our spirit serves as a conduit or connection between the natural world and the spiritual world.

Our soul, on the other hand, is the bridge of all our humanity. It, too, is eternal in nature, as far as things like our thoughts, decisions, and actions. They will all come with us for judgment.

Do you think our spiritual body in the spiritual world is similar to our natural body in this world?

Marcus Douglas

Chapter 2 – We Undoubtedly Are Its Soul

November 6th, 2024

The next day, the head of Dimensions thoroughly studied last night's successful apprehension of the Black Out report.

Natalie Massey, a Caucasian woman standing about five foot six, carried herself with a self-assured and upright posture. Eleven years ago, Natalie had been trained with four other lead psychics, or Enhanced, to be ready for an expansion. But their mentor and the founder of Dimensions, Brenden McDowell – who was a powerful Enhanced – mysteriously had to step down, just as they were picking up traction. That was when Natalie was thrusted into the position.

Dimensions was a hole-in-the-wall start-up with very little funding and close to no backing of any kind. Every form of law enforcement thought they were just a bunch of kids playing on the phones. Nine years ago, when Dimensions were very near to closing their doors, they caught a big break.

There was a prominent kidnapper named Zachariah Gross. He'd been traveling up and down the east coast, abducting three through six-year-old kids. The case didn't gain traction until a politician's six-year-old son was kidnapped.

Law enforcement had no leads. Zac was thorough and meticulous. He served five years in law enforcement, so he knew what they would be looking for. But a few at Dimensions had premonitions that Zac had an accomplice he depended on through their reign of terror. The accomplice – alias Lucifer – was maniacal and deranged. They did cataclysmic damage throughout Virginia.

Dimensions almost single-handedly led the FBI to their location. Not only that, they pointed law enforcement to the right places to find the bodies and evidence. It was a high-profile, very dire case.

They never caught Lucifer, though. A classic Guy Fawkes mask always covered their face, and the diamond wedding ring on their right hand was the only thing that could identify Lucifer, making the apprehension of the Lord of Darkness extremely difficult. The twins had vision after vision of Lucifer, but that detail was all they had. If it wasn't for that particular case, Dimensions would be a forgotten memory. It was a sad and chilling outcome, but one everybody was excited about it once it reached its conclusion.

After that point, Dimensions caught fire and took off. Now they had five buildings, and the main establishment worked directly for the government. And the new President had just mentioned them in his speech last night.

As Natalie was being driven to the Dimensions building by her car's AI function, as she carefully went over last night's enormous case.

"Beth," said Natalie.

The AI responded, "Yes, ma'am?"

"Call Charles Simmons," Natalie commanded.

"Calling."

The phone rang; a slightly older gentleman answered, "Good morning, Natalie."

"Good morning. Let's meet with the Chief Operating Officials of each branch in thirty minutes."

"Yes, ma'am," Charles said as he hung up.

Immediately after the call, Natalie slowly gazed out the window and reminisced at the small beginnings Dimensions and she had. Eleven years ago, Natalie was a lowly subjacent, learning the business from a powerful psychic named Brenden McDowell. She used to be so hopeful, extremely positive, and full of life. But her decisions had transformed her optimistic attitude to the woman she was today. Natalie didn't know how to care for people. The diabolical cases of Dimensions stole the glow from her soul. She had to fake a lot of emotions for the run-of-the-mill things that really were not important to her. Ever since the Zachariah Gross case, Natalie lived for Dimensions. No kids, no relationships. Dimensions was her significant other; the company had become her love child.

As building after building passed, her gaze became stoic. She reached down for her cup of warm tea. It wasn't just about where they came from or they were now, but where they were going. With an organization that had an impeccable reputation for seeing into the future, they were oblivious to their own. And that was the success and the demise of Natalie – she still feared the unknown. She shook her head, as though trying to dismiss the silent battle raging within. Natalie once doubted herself but definitely had a chance to take the keys to the kingdom and make the perfect future for her and Dimensions.

"Madam, we are here," said Beth.

The AI jolted Natalie out of her reverie and interrupted her thoughts. She grabbed her tablet, put it in her briefcase, and closed it.

She said, "I'm ready."

Right after, the statement prompted the upward motion of the suicide doors.

"Have a nice day, madam."

Natalie's stoicism drained from her face as she walked through the lobby. She stopped, taking in the vivacious scenery. The plush armchairs beckoned invitingly, and the soft hum of conversation floated gently in the air. A far cry from the cramped, dirty cubicles and muttered whispers where they'd started.

"Welcome to DOA, miss. How may I assist you today?" Beverly, one of their friendly receptionists, asked with a warm smile.

"Josephine Simms," she said as she returned the smile. "I'm here for a meeting with Mr. Johnson on the third floor."

Beverly nodded in understanding. "Of course, I'll notify him of your arrival. Feel free to help yourself to some refreshments while you wait."

She gestured towards a table laden with bagels, doughnuts, cobblers, strudels, and an array of fruit. The spread was massive, engulfing any of the visitors with instant appreciation for simply being present.

Josephine said, "Thank you," and made her way towards the refreshments, where another guest was already sipping from a cup.

Natalie watched from the entrance door, with a slight smirk.

"Quite the spread they have here, don't you think?" Josephine remarked, offering the receptionist some playful banter.

Beverly nodded in agreement. "Yes, it's quite impressive. Have you been here before?"

Josephine chuckled softly. "Oh, this is my second time. And each moment I feel a sense of belonging. DOA has a way of making me feel at home, don't you think?"

Beverly looked up and saw Natalie standing in the distance. "Good morning, Ms. Massey."

"Good morning, Beverly, how is your mother doing?"

Beverly surprised at the question, "Oh, well, she's doing better. Thank you for asking."

"No problem. Send her my prayers," Natalie said as she walked off.

"Good morning, Ms. Massey," said a series of workers.

Natalie responded with a happily fake, "Good morning."

Natalie got on the elevator, but she had a little time to kill and decided to go to Potential Hall.

Potential Hall boasted a prep room, specially designed to nurture the potentials who walked through its doors. Within these rooms laid an array of carefully curated elements aimed at fostering healthy sleep patterns and divine relaxation. From soothing scents that drifted through the air to plush furnishings that enveloped visitors in blissful comfort, every detail was crafted to create an environment conducive of self-discovery and healthy abilities.

The potentials were placed into two categories, Natural Ability Precipitant and the Enhanced Ability Precipitant. The people who fell under Natural Ability Precipitant were the ones who displayed psychic abilities without depending on drugs. They could have visions, premonitions, or dreams of future events with relative ease. The visions were within exact themes, such as dates, times, places, or people. Enhanced Ability Precipitants needed stimulants to provide comfort and feel like they transitioned to other worlds. Their vision was sketchy, but when thirty people had dreams about the same thing in different aspects, it provided a fuller picture.

The Natural Ability Precipitant, when Dimension first started, was the backbone of the establishment. The dreams and premonitions were pertinent but not as constant. It wasn't until they introduced the drug 114P6, and when it was approved by the FDA, that Dimensions started to take off. But there was a catch-22 – these types of visions were more constant but not consistent.

Denise Williams, one of the leads on the floor, was in her office talking to a potential named Claudia Davis about the opening steps of what Dimensions did.

Natalie walked up in the middle of the conversation.

Denise said, "Ms. Davis, I understand your concerns. But rest assured, every treatment we use has been rigorously tested and approved. We have a small medical facility right down the road, and they do extensive tests on potentials to make sure you are prepared. Then there are three months of training you must pass."

"Wow. So, it's not a quick fix; it takes time," said Claudia.

Denise nodded in agreement and continued, "That's correct, Claudia. It's definitely not short-term. We take our procedures very seriously to ensure the safety and accuracy of the information we provide."

Claudia was intrigued by Denise's explanation. "So, how do you differentiate between a psychic dream and a dream based on fear?"

Denise paused thoughtfully before responding, "It's a crucial distinction. A psychic dream often carries specific details or messages that are beyond what one would experience in a regular dream, whereas a dream based on fear tends to be more chaotic and emotionally charged."

Claudia nodded, absorbing the information. "That makes sense. So, what are some of the steps you take to validate the legitimacy of these visions?"

Denise smiled warmly, appreciating Claudia's interest. "Well, we have a stringent process in place that involves thorough documentation and verification from various sources within law enforcement and the judicial system. It's essential for maintaining the integrity of our work here at Dimensions."

Claudia's next question would pique a careful response. "Well, after a vision or a dream is revealed, what are the next steps?"

"That is a fabulous question, Ms. Davis. When a dream or vision or premonition is seen and verified as authentic, well, ma'am, it then goes up to the next floor called the Sifting," said Denise excitedly.

As their conversation continued, Denise delved into more detail about the training program and quality control measures that were implemented to ensure the accuracy and reliability of the psychic visions they provided. Claudia listened intently, gaining a deeper understanding of the intricate workings behind the scenes at Dimensions.

Natalie slowly closed her eyes to take in the aroma of success. She looked at her watch, and it was five minutes till the meeting. She proceeded back to the elevator and went up to the second floor.

She got out of the elevator and Charles, her assistant, and a woman greeted her with a bunch of governmental paperwork that needed Natalie's signature.

Charles said, "Ms. Massey, this is Joanne O'Neil. She will be your backup when I go out on surgery.

Natalie shook her hand. "It's nice to meet you, Joanne."

With her palms sweaty and her voice fluctuating, Joanne replied, "Uh, yes, why, yes, the pleasure is all mine."

"So, before you go in here, the wavier you sign – the suppression document – states that if you repeat or say anything from DOA meetings – classified documents or anything – you will be held to the highest levels of the law. Which will definitely mean lawsuits, but with us working directly under the government, it could mean prison. Joanne, the fail-safes are in place not only to protect the public from us, but more importantly, to protect us from the public. Can you imagine if one of our Enhanced's information got out to the world Anybody with a vendetta would be gunning for them. So, everything at DOA is monitored, from your emails to your phone records," said a stern Natalie.

Joanne nervously said, "Yes, ma'am."

"Relax, Joanne, you are with a company that can pierce into the future. If you weren't a right fit for us, we never would have hired you," said Natalie.

That statement terrified Joanne.

Natalie took the papers as they walked into the conference room. She gave Charles her tablet and told him to pull up last night's big case.

Joanne took a moment to admire the exquisite craftsmanship of the room.

"I must say, this conference room is truly a work of art," remarked Joanne, her voice filled with admiration. "I've never seen such a perfect blend of culture and technology before."

"I couldn't agree more," replied Charles, nodding in approval. "The attention to detail is impeccable. It's as if every element was carefully chosen to create an atmosphere of luxury and innovation."

"And let's not forget about the technology," he added. "That uni-synced live video chat system is a game-changer."

Natalie smiled at the lively discussion taking place around her. She was proud of the conference room she had a hand in its design, knowing that it not only provided a comfortable and elegant space for meetings but also embraced the cutting-edge advancements that would shape the future of business interactions.

"It combines traditionalism with state-of-the-art technology," Charles softly stated.

The heads of each department slowly appeared on the uni-synced video conference.

This technological wonder dominated one corner, seamlessly connecting individuals in real-time across digital platforms. Through this innovative technology, a digital enactment was brought to life, rendering a vivid 3D model that transcended physical boundaries. It was as if the actual person were present, even though they were miles away.

"Good morning, DOA," said Natalie.

The four acting head officials responded, "Good morning."

The team comprised the five individuals who had been trained by their mentor, Brenden McDowell. Everything they knew was based on Brenden's excellent teaching, which was considered the Holy Grail of the foundation of Dimensions. This team was known around DOA as the Fab Five.

"So, as you know, we had a case of monumental significance at the same time the President-elect was rehearsing our accolades to the nation. He has believed in what we do for as long as I can remember. With the new President as our biggest fan, and most notably you and your teams' dedication to hard work, it's only by you all we stand proudly where we are, so congratulate your team for me, please," said Natalie

The Dimensions members started to clap for one another. At the same time, Natalie reached for her tablet, only to find that it had frozen.

"I really wanted to discuss with you all the Black Out report in its totality. I know, you know what your particular department has done, but how does your team's individual success affect us as a whole?" asked Natalie

Donnie Smith said, "Well, Natalie, why don't we just go around the room and share what we've got? No need for the tablet."

Natalie said, "Okay, Donnie, what do you have for us?"

Donnie Smith, head of the North Dimensions, stood tall and confident in his tailored suit as his silly but charismatic charm captivated the room. He was known as the top psychic in his field and the chief Enhanced of the agency. Donnie's mastery of Dimensions made him the go-to person for all the major and high-profile court cases. But what truly fueled his passion was sharing his expertise with others. He regularly led seminars and trainings for law enforcement and youth groups, emphasizing the vital role of Dimensions in maintaining world stability. After over a decade with the agency, Donnie had established himself as a trusted and respected figure among his colleagues. To have Donnie's name associated with any project meant tapping into a wealth of knowledge and experience.

"So, about five months ago, we received our first vision from—" Donnie looked down at his paper "—subject ten-three-sixty-five in Dimensions Headquarters. It was a vivid dream with a vast number of deaths. The deaths came from a technological bomb known as IXG, which had immaculate and devastating capabilities on a mass scale. It became top priority when we had three matching dreams."

Joanne had a confused look on her face. And Charles noticed her blank expression.

He whispered, "What's wrong?"

"Why three?" Joanne whispered back.

Charles said, "The number three has biblical foundation. It means completeness."

"Well, after that, we turned over our findings to the Sniffers, I'm sorry, the Sifters," Donnie said as he snickered.

Pete said with a great deal of frustration, "Donnie, if it wasn't for us, half of you all's cases wouldn't have structure or a path, much less be seen by the courts as viable criminal charges."

Pete Alexander, a seasoned veteran of eight years, stood at the helm of the Sifters division within Dimensions of America. Despite being non-Enhanced, this team provided crucial structure and human element to the company. In 2017, a lawsuit threatened to ruin everything Dimensions had built. But thanks to the Sifters' work, both internally and externally, they were able to come out on top. With the company being full of Enhanced individuals, the fact that they had a non-Enhanced group was their saving grace.

Pete said, "When the third vision came, it hinted at a catastrophic tragedy. As usual, the Enhanced saw the destruction before they saw the when, where, and players involved. But we knew it was only a matter of time before we had everything we needed. It's really based on how trained the Enhanced are."

Donnie started to pop his collar, saying quietly but comically, "Thank you very much."

"Without them being highly trained on what things to look for as they traverse in a dream, vision, or premonition, everything would fall apart. Looking for street signs, clocks, and stopwatches. Looking for names, houses and addresses. It's a give-and-take; if the Enhanced are the body, the administration is the spirit, and we are undoubtedly its soul."

Pete continued, "Well, after knowing the when and where it's all about, do we have enough information to turn our findings over to the authorities? That will lead to their apprehension, but the question is, can we catch them in the act with no casualties? Or will there be blood spilled? It's like a puzzle board, and we are just placing in the right pieces. And when all the pieces are in place, it's time to send the info to the twins."

Monique and Dominique Russell were identical twin sisters, with long, curly black hair and sharp hazel eyes. They had been the first two Enhanced mentored by Brenden and still worked closely together in their roles. They were the other two Enhanced in the Zachariah Gross case. However, since getting married and having children, they traded the nightmarish prophecies for desk jobs. Monique dealt with local law enforcement, ATF, and

DEA. Dominique's focus was on federal agencies such as the FBI, Secret Service, and CIA. Despite their different specialties, they were one. They were known for finishing each other's sentences and predicting each other's next move without hesitation.

Monique said, "Yeah, getting the law involved, five years ago, used to be our most difficult challenge."

"Now, they're clamoring for our insight and expertise," said Dominique. "Once we presented them with the case and found out what division of the law we would be working under—"

Monique said on cue, "They were all fighting for this case, but it fell in the FBI's jurisdiction. We worked with them and set up the virtual presentation."

Dominique said, "And—"

Monique said, "—Voila."

"We got a warrant from Judge Ricardo Mathews to set wires and phone taps and put undercover officers in place," said Dominique.

Monique added, "The success was monumental with all involve parties. It definitely dives into the future of our ultimate goal."

"Yes, you're right, our level of organization, perseverance, and commitment should show that we are ready for our own legal department. Can you all imagine it?" Natalie paused in reverence. She could see the stars aligning, everything matriculating toward that goal.

Natalie said, "Thank you all for your hard work and dedication; this meeting is adjourned."

They started to talk among themselves, and then one after one, they logged off.

Donnie eyes darted around aimlessly. He swallowed hard, feeling the dryness in his throat and the sweat beginning to bead on his forehead. His foot tapped a restless rhythm on the floor, betraying the tension coiled within him. Donnie didn't know what he'd seen last night. He tried to convince himself it was just one dream.

Natalie looked at him. "Donnie, you're still here?"

"Yes, I have something that I need to talk to you about…" He paused and looked over at Charles and Joanne. "Sorry, guys, but privately."

With all Donnie's snickering, she always knew when he was troubled. Natalie said, "Can you take my things and put them in my office? Thank you."

Charles and Joanne immediately did what she asked and walked out, closing the door behind them.

"What do you have for me?" asked Natalie.

Donnie said, "I had a dream last night, a terrible, terrible dream."

"Well, Donnie, that's what we pay you for." She giggled to lighten the mood.

"Please, Natalie."

"Okay, what was the dream?"

"It was vivid. I was standing in front of the White House, and it's like, it's like my spirit left my body. I saw all the people standing outside, but they were saying something, but it was muted. But whatever the crowd were screaming, they yelled it with excitement. I floated into the Oval Office, and there were so many generals, key officials, and official delegates. When I floated in the door, I was behind the people. The man who was talking, I couldn't see his face, but I could hear his voice. And he was talking about murder, and death, so nonchalantly. Killing cities, massacring towns, bombing…"

His hands shook and the dryness in his throat started to overtake his fear of impending doom. "Bombing nations and the people are just cheering his name on the outside and in. When I finally made way through the crowd, it was President-elect Franklin Adams. Then they all were cheering his name, 'Adams, Adams.' Then I woke up. My God, I still get sweaty thinking about it."

"Well, Donnie, this is my first documentation of our President committing genocide. Have you recorded it into your log yet?" asked Natalie.

"No, not yet."

"Well, I'll take care of it and put it down for you. I just think, given the delicacy of this matter, it's best if this is an issue I personally handle."

"You're right. And I'll get it to you first thing in the morning."

"Have a good remainder of the day."

"You too, Natalie." said Donnie

Natalie watched Donnie's body totally disintegrate into nothingness until the spot where his computer image had stood was now a simple "call disconnected."

Natalie walked into her office, sat down at her desk, and let out a heavy sigh.

She rose gracefully from her plush office chair, her sharp eyes trained on the concealed panels behind her desk. The wall looked deceptively simple, but it held a secret only

Natalie knew. Made of sleek black marble with a glossy finish, it reflected everything in its surroundings with impeccable precision. The hidden filing cabinet was a marvel of engineering, its electronic locking mechanism providing unparalleled security for its contents. Within the cabinet lay countless classified files and secrets that even Natalie's most trusted colleagues were unaware of.

She reached in the bottom draw, in which lay sixteen different documented dreams of the DOA witnessing the President-elect committing mass murder.

Overture 3 – Mediator

The term "mediator" is a person who attempts to help people involved in a conflict come to an agreement, a go-between. Their influence on all situations entailed is critical. *Just as a lawyer mediates in legal matters, our soul acts as a mediator in the constant dialogue between our body and spirit.* They would have all the knowledge and bring the case to a justifiable outcome.

It gives the information to and from the body and spirit. For example, if you are dealing with lust, it is something that your body is yearning for; however, your spirit is sorely against. As I'm writing this story, my church is in the month of consecration, which means we arc fasting. Now, watch this: my body tells my soul that we are hungry, and my soul passes that message to my spirit. But my spirit is saying we are fasting, and sadly, my soul informs my body, and it falls in line.

Just as a lawyer mediates for justice, the soul mediates between body and spirit. Jesus Christ became the ultimate mediator, bridging the gap between humanity and salvation through His sacrifice on the cross.

Marcus Douglas

Chapter 3 – It Was One from the Depths of His Very Soul

November 13th, 2024

Something has changed, thought Sharron Adams, the newly appointed First Lady.

She gazed at her husband, both privileged to the horrible news that would shatter their entire existence. This was not like receiving a terminal diagnosis. With those, you can attempt to put up some type of fight. But a prophecy that predicts you will make terrible decisions of the greatest magnitude is inevitable to run from.

As Adams tightened his grip on Sharron's hand, it majestically transformed into a signal that only she and Adams could decipher. An unconscious plea of the complex variety that simply yells out, *I can't do this on my own*. A cry, if you will, that goes past his thoughts and emotions, it was one from the depths of his very soul. But on the surface, Adams looked like he was handling the news extremely well.

The White House chief physician, Eric Atkins; the head doctor of psychological studies, Brett Swanson; and Natalie, the head of Dimensions, stood in the White House medical room. The attempts to carefully explain what they found were like a series of dominos. One discovery after the next made their doubts very much real. However, it was all background noise to Sharron when her mind went back to the first time she met Adams eight years ago.

September 17th, 2015

The Marquee Sunset was renowned for its enchanting atmosphere and exceptional fine dining. Every detail exuded lavishness, from the sparkling tableware to the radiant chandeliers adorned with diamonds. Rumors said the glass floors were crafted from these gems, providing a mesmerizing view of decadent dishes being prepared. The three-story sanctuary also featured a level dedicated to vintage furniture, each piece telling its own story of extravagance.

"Excuse me, excuse me, have you ladies voted for Senator Conway? There are a lot of issues that are facing young, attractive women like yourselves. Your vote could be the deciding factor in this year's election." Adams was talking really fast and with heightened nervousness but somehow remained confident.

One of Sharron's friends, Nykki Simmons, spoke comically, "Sir, do you not know where you are?"

Adams knew exactly where he was, but Sharron was so beautiful and God-awfully stunning, he couldn't let this opportunity slip away.

Conversations angrily surrounded the table where they were sitting.

"He's doing this at a restaurant? The audacity! Somebody call the police!"

"Sir, I am way too drunk to understand what you are saying, but you are cute, though," Sharron said as she giggled. *Now why did I just say that?*

"I think you're undoubtedly gorgeous," Adams said as he leaned in, mesmerized by her light brown eyes.

"Oh my God, wake up, girl! He knows who you are. That's why he started talking about politics," Nykki said as she sighed.

Sharron Carpenter was the youngest daughter of George and Cassandra Carpenter. George was a prominent real estate tycoon-turned-governor for two terms, and Cassandra was the United States Attorney General. Sharron had graduated from law school but also had minored in public speaking. Her family was a very big deal in Washington.

The officers at the entrance of the restaurant begin talking to one of the servers, trying to get an understanding of what was going on. The waiter tried to explain vigorously with his hands and then pointed at Adams.

"Your friend is right. I know exactly who you are. You are my future wife." It was so authentic, so spur of the moment.

The alcohol put her emotions on overdrive – it was like his words pierced through her soul.

The officers came into the luxurious establishment. "Alright, sir, time for you to leave."

Adams refused as he asked Sharron, "Would you go out with me?"

The cop yelled, "Sir, this is your final warning. I said leave!"

Sharron was taken aback from everything going on and was left speechless.

The cop said, "Alright, son, let's go downtown."

Adams put his hands behind his back to be arrested, as if he knew the outcome of his decision.

The officers started to walk him out the restaurant doors.

Nykki said, "Thank God those officers showed up when they did. Waiter, waiter!"

"Yes, how can I serve you?" asked the server.

But Sharron was deep in thought. What if this was the love she had always longed and hoped for?

Sharron jumped up out of her seat, knocking it to the floor. She bolted to the exit, trying to catch the cops before they pulled off. She ran outside, high heels clicking, and wrote her phone number on a napkin.

"When you get out of jail, call me," she said, sliding her number inside his back pocket.

Adams was extremely excited as the officers pulled off.

Present Day

Everybody who stood before the President-elect and his wife didn't want to disclose the dire news, but this wasn't about one man. This was about the United States as a whole. If this prophecy was true, it would be devastating for the entire country.

Sharron was distraught, her emotions all over the place. Although similar to the President-elect, she kept her true emotions bottled up. While the First Lady stared at her husband, her lips trembled slightly.

When they first met, Adams was moved by his emotions, but now nothing really moved him emotionally. He knew how to keep his composure when everyone around him was losing theirs. It was one of the reasons he would make a great President. However, this crushing news would be Adams's demise. The doctors and Natalie attempted to inform Adams and his wife about their discovery delicately. It was unsuccessful at every turn.

Sharron was terrified as well as relieved that this horrible situation had occurred. An evil prognosis of astronomical proportions, she felt awful for feeling good that the prophecy would make him depend on her. It would make him need her. It gave her life purpose. Sharron stared at her husband and once again reminisced about when she started feeling like their relationship was changing.

October 11th, 2017

Sharron sat in their immaculate home in suburban Maryland. The magnificent three-story home was a masterpiece gifted to them on their wedding day by Sharron's dad. Its classical design, with burnt-orange and red brick and smoke-gray accents, exuded elegance. The 4,933-square-foot house was both spacious and grand, blending old-world charm with modern sensibilities. Inside, warm colors created an inviting atmosphere for comfort and relaxation.

Sharron sat in their office, finishing up some consultant paperwork for her firm, George and Lee, Attorneys at Law. She needed it finished before four p.m. and was way ahead. It was only nine a.m., and she was almost done. Sharron really enjoyed being a consultant; it allowed her to be flexible and pick her own cases and clients. Nevertheless, Sharron needed to be done because it was her husband's big day. He'd been nominated for a Nobel Peace Prize. And who better to speak about his accomplishments than her?

To think he was just co-head of President Conway's campaign in Washington, D.C., four years ago. Now, he was on par with winning one of the most prestigious honors. But Adams had been extremely nervous all week.

Indecisive about his wardrobe, unsure about tonight's speech. With all the confidence to be put in these positions, it was like his self-assurance depleted as his fear increased. In his mind, nothing was going right. So, he took a morning jog to clear his thoughts. To release some frustration and relax. Before he walked out, he talked about needing his wife's input on some crucial matters.

Adams walked through the door of the house. Sharron was excited to see him – after reading her speech, she was so proud of everything he had persevered through.

Adams walked through the door, he yelled out a playful, "Lucy, I'm home."

He strolled into their office and kissed his wife on the cheek.

"Hey, my love, how'd the run go?" Sharron picked her head up quickly and then went back to finishing her work.

Adams walked into the kitchen to get a drink. "Oh, it was perfect. Exactly what I needed."

She finished the final touches on her consultation form, then proceeded to walk up the stairs.

Sharron said, "Kirk, Kirk…"

But Adams remained quiet.

Sharron's footsteps went from a hurry to a slight cautiousness in a matter of seconds. An eerie feeling went down her spine, as if she was an actress in a horror movie.

"Alright, Kirk, this is not funny," she called in fear. Sharron's heartbeat through her chest. Her emotions started taking control, she was careful, but a wave of concern had taken precedence as well.

Sharron arrived at their room and was looked for Adams' body to be collapsed on the floor or gasping for dear life, but when she fully walked into the room, she saw her husband staring in front of the bathroom mirror. He had a weird gaze that was enhanced the longer he looked at himself. As though he didn't recognize the face that looked back at him. A stranger in his own body, a traveler in his very skin.

"Kirk!" Sharron yelled.

"Did you not hear me calling you?" she added with concern.

He snapped out of his trance. "I'm sorry, hon, I got caught up in my mind. There's a million things to do," he said as he began to grin.

"You seemed to be in a much happier space; it's like night and day," said Sharron.

Adams said jovially, "I guess that jog did me well. You would be amazed how much some exercise will do the body good."

"Alright, so let's get to these suits," said Sharron.

"Yeah, no, I got it. I'm going to do the traditional black classic Tom Ford," Adams responded as he pulled the suit out of the closet and sat it on the bed.

"Hon, you said the Tom Ford was too bland and old-fashioned. And now you're sure that this is the suit?" asked a perplexed Sharron.

"It's a classical event; why not go retro?" He grinned again.

"Okay, so… let's move on to your speech. Now, I think—"

Adams interrupted, "Oh, I'm sorry, hon. I decided to go with the speech that promotes taking care of the incarcerated. I think that speech will wake people up of the dangers facing our imprisoned."

"Kirk, Kirk, wasn't this speech at the bottom of your list? Now you're saying that's the one you are picking. You don't even want me to listen to other ones," pleaded Sharron.

Adams said, "No, I feel confident that it's the right speech. The right message for the right time."

"Okay, well, I guess my work here is done," Sharron said as she laughed at her own joke.

But Adams didn't laugh; he just continued to spread that heinous grin.

Sharron paid her husband's weird behavior no never mind. Not until their next conversation.

Sharron picked up a magazine off the bed. "Oh, I was reading this article. It talked about dreams and your soul. It had a lot of good quotes. Like, it said your soul emulates your dreams and vice versa."

She skimmed through the page and asked, "Yes, it had a lot of quotes. What do you think?"

Adams sat on the floor, cross-legged, shining his shoes. He appeared oblivious to her question. Adam gave complete concentration on the task at hand.

"Kirk, are you listening to me? Kirk, Kirklin'?" she repeatedly called.

But he had zoned out, extremely focused on shining his shoes. Sharron let him be, walking downstairs to the kitchen to get some cranberry juice, when she saw the half-drunken cup.

Sharron yelled, "Hon, don't forget to put your cup in the…" Her voice tapered off as what she realized was concerning.

"Kirk!" she yelled as she hurried up the stairs with the half cup of orange juice.

She made it up the stairs and spewed out, "Hon, your acid reflux – you can't be drinking orange juice…"

When she came into the bedroom, Adams was standing directly at the door. It startled her, and he started talking like that was the norm.

"Hon, I don't have dreams," said Adams softly.

Sharron said out of concern, "What do you mean, you don't have dreams?"

He closed his eyes, as if he could physically see what he was explaining. "Well, I have dreams, but they're not meaningful. I have the same recurring dream. I am in this house; there is nothing really significant. When I walk outside, there is this massive space, but it's all enclosed in by a wall."

Adams started to tear up as he continued, "I walk for hours, feeling like something is important inside the walls. And it's always the same dream, tormenting me."

Sharron felt her husband's sadness and immediately coincided with his pain. She hugged him. "Honey, I'm so sorry."

Present Day

Senator Carter sat in his limousine, watching the President-elect's test, and the heinous prophecy, all via webcam. He was severely disappointed. This not only ruined the President's life, but everything Carter put forth to secure this outcome was slowly fading away. The senator had put so much time and money into Adams. He'd heard about this same prophecy years ago. Carter thought the man was clout chasing or just trying to get a significant amount of fame, but maybe he could take a step back and regroup and then, after four years, try at it again.

Sharron gazed at Adams, her mind jolting back to the day when everything had changed. It was the moment she realized he no longer needed her. She felt like nothing more than a beautiful decoration, meant for show and appearances, rather than using her God-given abilities. Even their physical intimacy lacked any passion or depth – it had become routine. A simple good night and good morning. Her husband had once mentioned his dreams feeling meaningless, but in the past seven years of marriage, she too had begun to feel her life was devoid of meaning. She had prayed for a reason to continue fighting, and now this… this unexpected turn of events had occurred.

The President-elect paused during his questioning, "How will the American people react to this? What about my family and friends? What about my parents? They will be devastated. How is, how is this even plausible?" Adams' voice filled with nervousness and fear.

Natalie asked, "Sir, have you ever had reason to doubt Dimensions?"

"No, ma'am, you all have been the bright spot in… I just, I, I just can't believe that me, I would be a mass murderer," Adams said, confused.

Dr. Swanson said, "Sir, the data is accurate. We did a brain scan, and it matched ninety-eight percent with the people that experience what we call psychosis unrest."

"Psy-what, unrest-what? You don't have to dress it up, Doc, you can call it crazy!" said Adams, climbing angrily from his seat.

Adkins said, "Calm down, Mr. President. I didn't want to believe it either. The supernatural, prophecies, and psychic abilities are hogwash compared to science – no offense, Natalie – but the science is pinpoint accurate, and the supernatural confirms the science. It seems like the first time everything is going hand-in-hand, a healthy medium. It's just terrible that destiny has chosen you as its morning star."

Adams' breath hitched, his knees buckling under the weight of the truth. Sharron wrapped her arms around him to attempt to mend his broken heart.

Adams said softly, looking at his wife with tears in his eyes, "I'm going to have to resign my position."

Those words triggered his emotions as he cried profusely.

"Is there anything we can do?" asked Sharron emotionally while she continued to console her husband.

"No, ma'am, for the safety of everybody, the only thing he could do is step down," said Adkins.

Natalie's heart hung heavy for the President-elect, but this was exactly the storm she had prayed for. Just like the Zachariah Gross case, it could propel Dimensions ahead into the sunset. Her dreams and ambitions could not have concocted a more perfect plan. If there was one thing that Dimensions did, it was change the future, and she would fake whatever emotions, deplete her soul however she had to, to make sure everyone saw exactly that. She played every situation like a game of chess, and, when it seemed like all hope was lost, made a suggestion out of left field.

Natalie said, "Wait, wait, what if your resigning is the catapult that sends you over the edge?"

Everybody in the room immediately pulled their heads up.

Natalie had a sly smile. "I know of a place that could be good for this specific brand of work. If we can just change, and counteract, what the science says that's in your character, then we can change this prophecy completely."

Sharron asked, "What is this place?"

Senator Carter watched, steaming mad, because he knew there was only one place that specialized in what Natalie would suggest. And to keep his secrets hidden – and him not brought up on several criminal charges – the inner workings had to remain a secret.

"Mr. President, have you ever heard of a place called Alora's Dream Haven?" said a confident Natalie.

Overture 4 – Deposit

A deposit is a layer or body of accumulated matter. We mostly think of deposits as financial, but anything that involves safe keeping, or reuseable substance, can be deposited. Teachers, scholars, and parents deposit knowledge into your mind, shaping your understanding and growth. But beyond them, life itself also makes deposits, sometimes in ways we least expect.

In this case, the deposit has two parts, the knowledge that the senses deposit into the soul and what the soul deposits into the body and spirit. Our senses act as silent messengers, feeding the soul with information that influences our decisions. They all run so fluidly that they are barely noticed. How something was heard, or how it smelled, or tasted, what you saw, and what it felt – that information is deposited into your soul. And then the soul deposits it into your body and spirit to perform an action. Your body is screaming, "Yes, this feels so good," but your spirit is saying, "No, this is not in the will of God." And your soul thus makes the decision.

What have you allowed to be deposited in your soul lately?

Marcus Douglas

Chapter 4 – Conceal Her Memories Inside Her Soul

November 19th, 2024

"Good morning, Mr. President, Mrs. Adams. Welcome to Alora's Dream Haven. I'm Jamie Bradshaw, your liaison. How was your trip to Escondido?"

The President-elect said, "We are doing good, and it was well; thank you for asking."

"I'm so happy to hear that. So, if you all have any questions or comments about our great facility, don't hesitate to ask. I talked to your assistant, Margret, who said you're interested in the full tour. Am I correct with that assessment?" she asked.

"Yes, that is correct," Adams said as he looked at his wife with a hint of nervousness.

"Well, if you all follow me, I can start this presentation. Alora's Dream Haven has been a staple in the community for fourteen years now. The vision all started by two African doctors. Cudjoe Uma, he was the brilliant scientist, and Ashanti Eve, who was the local doctor. They both, through medicine and science, stumbled across each other through a mutual patient. They soon realized that, through their methods, they were the missing pieces to each other's work. Together, they made leaps and bounds, feeding off each other's concepts and ideals. To think, we once started from a little hole-in-the-wall facility, and now we are a three-hundred-million-dollar-a-year establishment! This is our only building at the moment, but we're looking at venturing outside of the States," said Jamie, like she was reading directly from a pamphlet.

Sharron asked, "The building is phenomenal. What's keeping you from expanding?"

"Let's just say a situation has occurred that has put us in a position where we have to show more perseverance," responded a reserved Jamie.

Adams and Sharron looked at each other with a plethora of uncertainty as they rode up to the third floor. They all got off the elevator as Jamie continued with the tour.

"So, our owners are the highly popular English gangster rapper, the Decipha, who owns 42% of the company; the other is an Italian billionaire named Benedetta Forte, who owns 39%. The president of the company is none other than its founder, Ashanti Eve, who you'll see shortly," she said as they walked up on a gentleman.

He was Caucasian, in his mid-forties, standing about five foot eleven. Cedrick Clemmons was his name, and he was the Chief Legal Officer.

Jamie said, "I'm going to turn you over to Mr. Clemmons, our CLO, who will continue the rest of your tour."

Sharron turned to Cedrick. "Mr. Clemmons, let me ask you something. How are you able to keep this place thriving if it's so very hard to find?"

She presented the question with a series of convictions. Cedrick laughed off the stern look. "Oh, Madam Adams, we have contracts that keep the finances flowing."

She looked back at the President-elect and gave an exaggerated laugh. Adams looked at Sharron with comical confusion.

"So, if you're making so much money annually, it should be easy to branch out. What's stopping you, really?" asked a determined Sharron.

Cedrick hesitantly said, "Just a couple of small missteps, nothing big."

He was about to send Jamie off when Sharron arched an eyebrow. "Would this have anything to do with China and India pulling out of resent negotiations?"

Jamie's face was pale, while Cedrick shifted uncomfortably.

"Mr. Clemmons, my mother served two terms as Attorney General, and my father was a well-known governor. We have friends in high places that are privileged to information such as this. And when your track record comes to the forefront of the conversation, I can only assume that your failures are hidden in the back. And so, in order for us to continue, we'll have to be totally candid with each other."

Cedrick blurted, "How do you know about that? We had very strict governmental documents that prevented anybody from disclosing that information."

Sharron pointed at Adams as she kept her eyes on Cedrick. "Do you know who this man is? This is not somebody who stumbled into this building fresh off the streets. This is the President of the United States. What single person has more influence than him? What he says or doesn't say can make or break this company. And, seeing that you just fell out of favor with India and China, the President-elect being at Alora's is an enormous opportunity for this establishment."

"Ma'am, Mr. President, from a legal standpoint, I can't disclose…" Cedrick stopped mid-sentence.

"Yes, ma'am. But the legal ramifications will be significant. Yes, yes, ma'am." Cedrick all of a sudden talked to the small earpiece in his ear. "We'll tell you everything you want to know," he said as he ushered his hand down the hall.

The President-elect softly grabbed Sharron's hand and persisted with Cedrick down the hall. Adams bubbled with laughter on the inside, while Sharron started to get teary-eyed. She remembered how it felt to be important in her husband's life once again. Sharron tried to hide her emotions, package up her feelings, and conceal her memories inside her soul.

"Thank you, Jamie," Cedrick said as she bowed and walked off. "So, you all have to promise me none of this information I'm about to tell you goes beyond us?"

They nodded in agreement.

Cedrick closed his eyes. "Alora's Dream Haven has had its fair share of hiccups. Ashanti and Cudjoe started to fall for one another and even got married. That love for one another pushed their work to new heights. When they figured out the way to Dream Walk in one another's dreams using technology, it was a game changer."

Adams asked, "Dream Walk, what's that?"

"It's when two people transfer a syncing of two brain patterns, which in turn forms a connection. Doctor Ashanti found this bridge in our hippocampus that spans the gap mentally between users and instantaneously allows one user to connect to the other's mind. She called it the Daraja. Once the Daraja has connected the users, the Stasis Traveling in Hope, or Dream Walk, can be performed.

Sharron asked, "Wait a minute, you guys have found a way to enter other people's dreams?"

"We can do that and so much more," Cedrick said as he swiped his card on one of the doors.

The President-elect bellowed, "Wow, look at this place!"

They laid eyes on this technological wonder, this state-of-the-art facility that was a sanctuary for weary souls, offering an escape from the chaos in a series of rooms known as Tulia. Its sleek design and futuristic architecture drew whispers of awe from those who beheld its beauty.

Within these hallowed walls, one could find a haven like no other. Rows upon rows of seat-like massage recliners beckoned patients to sink into their plush embrace, providing a cocoon of comfort and serenity. As the recliners enveloped their weary bodies, a sense of weightlessness embraced them, transporting them to a realm akin to zero-gravity. It was an experience that transcended reality itself, where the solace of the room transformed mere sleep into a delightful symphony of tranquility.

Gone were the days of small data pads awkwardly placed on one's head. In this modern age, the headrests at Alora's Dream Haven offered relaxation with just a simple act – laying one's head back against its heavenly cushion. As if by some magical force, tension melted away from weary minds, and with each breath, the dreamers were swept away into the most peaceful slumber imaginable. But this place held more than just dreams and relaxation; it held secrets about one's character that would undoubtedly be altered and would shape a person's destiny.

"Mrs. Adams, you asked, 'Are we able to enter each other's dreams?' What Dr. Eve and Cudjoe were able to do was extraordinary. Their focus started with making this phenomenal technology that allowed a person to directly visualize imagery of a person's dream. The concept, if achieved, would work wonders for sleep therapy and many other sleep aids. And they *were* successful. However, the technology was way ahead of its time. Imagine if you had the capabilities to view somebody's dream?"

President Adams asked, amazed, "How is that possible?"

"Well, sir, the good doctor and Cudjoe created a combination of medicine and technology that directly affects the small part of our brain called the occipital lobe. The medicine increases the electric receptors, and the technology hijacks the visual nature of the occipital."

"But with no audio, right? I would think that this would be totally visual, seeing that you need your ears to hear," stated the President confidently.

Cedrick said, "Yes and no. You see, your brain has extensive functions that feed off of one another. So, yes, your hearing is important in reality. If you can't hear in this world, then the effect becomes cataclysmic – if you can't hear, then you can't speak. If you can't speak, then it becomes difficult to learn. But think, in your dreams, the sound is not happening through your ears but through your mind. Your brain has carefully gelled sounds, with positions, of what it is and what the sound should display.

If you drop a metal fork on a tile floor, based on reality, your mind remembers what that sounds like. So, in the dreamscape, all it needs is your memory. Your memory is the key to your dreams concerning sound."

The President-elect was like a kid in a candy store, soaking in every word like a sponge.

"What's in the vials of tubes connected to the machines?" asked Sharron.

"The medicine in the vials is called Zulu. It's totally safe and FDA approved. There were several different interactions of the drug that Dr. Cudjoe and Dr. Eve also implemented. It enhances the mind, making the brain waves stronger and also makes the bridge that connects the minds more powerful," Cedric responded.

The President-elect reclined in one of the many seats, laid his head back, and let out a relaxing, "These things are comfortable."

"The headrest are the bulk of our technology; just one of these devices costs $200,000, and we have fifty of them in just this room. We have four floors," said Cedrick.

Adams asked as he got up, "This all sounds very expensive to operate, and, seeing that you all are not in the yellow pages, how do you bring in so much cash annually?"

"As I was saying earlier, we have a lot of contracts, especially military. You have to think, Mr. President, we demand a lot from the people that protect our country. Being among all that killing and all that war, then thrust them back into civilian existence – it's not fair to ask. However, what if before they returned, they could come here and get therapy? And enter the world right as rain?" asked a solemn Cedrick.

Sharron asked, "So, what does therapy look like for them?"

"That's an excellent question that progresses us into the next part of the tour." Cedrick took his keycard and swiped it into a more secluded room.

They walked into a room with a glass wall separating the patient's room from where they were. There was a patient and a therapist in back-to-back chairs.

"So, try to follow me. This is going to sound weird at first, but the more I talk, the more it's going to make perfectly good sense. When you dream, things may be different, but your mind bases your dreams on the concept of reality. Now, in your dream, you may be able to fly or manipulate matter, but that's one in a million. The basis of your dream is being in some sort of construct. Houses, homes, or buildings are in every dream, whether you realize it or not. Mrs. Adams, in the last dream you had, was there one of the three?" asked Cedrick.

Sharron responded, "Now that you say it, I don't really know."

"I know it's trippy. Houses are so common that your mind looks at it as typical, but they play a very important part in your psyche.

"So, imagine that your specific home in the dreamscape was a symbol of your human body in the dream world. I present to you all Second Lieutenant John Doe. He was leading a squad when one of his men stepped on a land mine. The shrapnel killed everyone in his squad. Miraculously, he survived. But, when trying to escape, he stepped on a land mine as well. The second lieutenant had to stand there for three days. He survived, but it caused irreparable damage to his psyche. His fear made him afraid to walk, and it became so deeply embedded in his subconscious, it convinced his physical body that his mind and his will were depleted." Cedrick told the story like he was at the lieutenant's tragic event.

The President-elect said, "How are you changing him?"

"Well, Mr. President, we sent in a specialized sleep therapist known as an Ubuntu Joiner. So, just like if you make changes to your body, there is a lot of work that goes behind it. Let's say if you want to work on the flaws in your character. People like child molesters, who are good but can't control their despicable hunger. Then Ubuntu goes in and assesses what type of therapy is needed. Now, due to legal obligations, we can't share the footage on lieutenant Doe," said Cedrick.

The President-elect and Sharron were glued to every syllable that proceeded from the CLO's mouth. The President-elect, especially, held on to every word like a newborn baby fighting for its mother's warmth. A thought that was in the back of his mind, now moved to the front, and that was hope.

"Dream Augmented Sleep Therapy, or DAST, is a successful alignment that allows the Ubuntu, or therapist, to go in and present the patient with a strong suggestion. In Lieutenant Doe's case, that's telling him he was brave and honorable. There is no need to fear, because you are safe. What happened in battle needs to stay in battle. You can walk, with confidence, with purpose and assurance," Cedrick continued as they looked at the lieutenant.

"Now, for our extreme cases, there is a therapy that is called the Dream Allurement Stasis. DAS. It's when the patient's brain waves are not responding to the change, and the Ubuntu must redirect the adjustment, and whatever the focus was on, to secure it in a room the patient no longer has access to. Have you ever heard of sweeping things under the rug? Just imagine the rug as a room. Sometimes it can be a door, gate, or metal bars, and the Ubuntu convinces the patient that they don't have power to access that particular room," Cedrik said as he brought his gaze back on the lieutenant and continued.

"A person with strong fears or wills, someone who has let the thing that needs to be fixed to set root and grow, needs to have the situation trapped and not changed. Think, how would it feel for you to have a struggle that can be magically fixed with about three or four sessions? Something that you have been warring against for years?"

As the lieutenant's final session ended, he, and the Ubuntu woke up. The Ubuntu stood, and the lieutenant sat on the side of the chair and let out a mighty yawn. And proceeded to stand up, the miracle of now being able to walk a sight for sore eyes. The lieutenant started to cry as all the fear and doubt washed away. He got so emotional that he dropped to his knees.

Adams' hope had grown exponentially. He got closer and put his hand up on the glass toward the lieutenant. It was like Adams could feel the lieutenant's fear turning into relief. Oh, how he wanted that feeling for himself.

Sharron walked slowly towards her husband and softly laid her hand on his back. Adams had leaned his head down and started sniffling. He looked back up at the lieutenant and said quietly, "This is it."

Sharron said, "Yes, but no human system is perfect. Come on. Let's continue and ask a few more questions."

She gently took his hand.

Cedrick pulled out his keycard and let them through some double doors, which led back to the elevator. They went towards the top floor.

"The infrastructure here is amazing, but what aren't you telling us?" asked the President-elect.

Cedrick let out a deep sigh. "Does the name 'Demario Evans' sound familiar?"

"Yes, the convict who went to prison at eighteen," said the President-elect. "He got thirty years for manslaughter, attempted murder, and aggravated assault. Demario tried to kill his parents because they stole illegal drugs from him. He got on a program that completely turned his life around and started to be a beacon of hope within the cell. They let him out six years early for good behavior. Once out, Demario immediately went to his parents' house and shot them dead, then killed himself right after. A very sad story."

They proceeded off the elevator to the top floor.

Cedrick began the story with a plethora of disappointment. "Mr. Evans would be our prized accomplishment. When he went to Lewisburg Penitentiary on a thirty-year sentence, he was spiraling and picking up steam. He got in with the gang known as the Dark Phantoms and was task to eliminate one of the leaders of the Mexican gangs, Juan Diego.

"They met in the yard. Evans shanked Juan Diego twice but didn't kill him. Through Juan's rehabilitation, he was sent to Alora's, and we changed his character. The warden had heard of our successful work with inmate patients through mutual friends. He wanted to make Alora's a part of their rehab, so we turned his life around. But we could only do so much with Juan Diego, because, in his mind, his dwelling place was only so big."

"I'm sorry, what do you mean by 'so big'?" asked Sharron.

"His mind's holding ground of memories," A woman interrupted with a Swahili accent.

"Mr. President and Mrs. Adams, I would like to introduce you all to the great Ashanti Ayo Okoye Eve, MD, PhD," said Cedrick.

"Please, Doctor Eve will suffice," she said candidly as she shook their hands.

"Have we met? Your face looks so familiar," asked a confused Adams.

Dr. Eve said, surprised, "Yes, why, yes, I was at the event when you won the Nobel Peace Prize. Your speech on reforming the prison population really moved me to start working with the inmates. We should put some of our resources together after the tour. Thank you, Mr. Clemmons."

Cedrick bowed out gracefully as Dr. Eve continued exactly where Cedrick left off

"Did you all used to play hide and seek?" asked Dr. Eve.

Both Adamses responded, "Yes."

"So, it's harder to hide in a small space, and it's easier to hide in an enormous space. This is the same with the dream world. With Juan Diego's house, it was a small, beat down shack. We were able to give him suggestions that he responded well to and that changed him for the better, and we were able to hide some stuff, and Juan Diego was a new man, so to speak. So, the warden recommended that we take their extremely bad apples.

"Mr. Evans was one of the ten. When we went into his mind, his lapa – which is Swahili for 'house' – was a mansion. By far the second biggest home I've ever seen. We knew we could make incredible strides with Evans. And so, we did. It was so magnificent," Dr. Eve said as she directed them into her office.

The President-elect and Sharron came in the room and sat down.

"So, I studied Mario's case carefully. It said a lot but nothing about Alora's being remotely involved," said Adams.

The doctor sat down. "Demario's case was assured by me and my staff. Alongside myself, I put my most seasoned Ubuntu, Passion Taylor, on the case. We put a lot of faith into the success of the transformation of Mr. Evans. The outside world didn't know we were directly involved. That's why there was very little about our participation. But his revenge was so embedded in his heart that he found a room to hide his hatred for his mother and father that we carelessly overlooked. Demario showed us exactly what we needed to see. He played with Passion's emotions. Oh God, she wanted to see the be—"

She interrupted herself. "We all wanted to see the best in him. When he killed his parents, everyone in this company was heartbroken, especially Ms. Passion. She looked at him like a son, and he used that love. Demario was every bit of a criminal. We had gotten India and China to sign a gag order, but we assured them we didn't need it. Our confidence blinded us. Our assurance betrayed us. That gag order was the only thing that didn't allow everything to blow out of proportion."

"Love, this could really work! They could really fix me!" said Adams.

Sharron let out a concern. "Yes, more than likely, however, the risk is too high."

"Wait, what are we talking about?" asked Dr. Eve.

Sharron let out a cautious, "Baby, what if they can't fix what's wrong?"

The President-elect let out an emotional, "There is nothing else I have to lose."

Sharron thought within herself the answer to that heartfelt question was simply... *me*.

"Mr. President, Mrs. Adams, even with our more than secretive failure, we still have a very high track record of completion. Tell me what the issue is, and we can walk through it," said Dr. Eve.

President-elect Adams looked at the doctor and said, "Death on a mass level."

And those words immediately put a cold chill down Dr. Eve's spine.

Overture 5 – Emotion

The emotions of man are very vital to our soul. They were created to be an enhancer of our feeling. Even Jesus got emotional. Before He raised Lazarus from the dead, He cried. Just hours before His crucifixion, He broke down and started crying once He saw His future. He even was riddled with anger when he saw His disciples sleep before his crucifixion. So, you see, emotion was never a mistake. It's important that we are not controlled by emotion. This is why fasting is so important. Spiritually, it brings you closer to God. But naturally, it teaches your body subjugation. It controls your yearning and quenching and gives a phenomenal decoration that tells your emotions, "I have power over you."

When is a particular moment you gave into your emotion, good or bad?

Marcus Douglas

Chapter 5 – His Character, His Mannerism, His- His Soul

November 20th, 2024

Senator Carter made many sacrifices to push Adams' future to the forefront. Carter played a hand in every significant alteration in the President-elect's life, but how far, and to what degree, did his involvement warrant?

Senator Carter got an important text message from the VP of Alora's, saying, "We are taking the President-elect on as a patient."

Carter had a mixture of fright, disbelief, and anger. His mouth dropped, as he had been unequivocally guaranteed that the President-elect would not be admitted to Alora's. Senator Carter was very keen on keeping his distance from Adams. But with the revealing of this prophecy, and now the President-elect being a patient at Alora's, the situation had become dire. It would be a race against the very essence of time. But if the truth came to the surface, he would be indicted on numerous charges.

On the other end of the spectrum was Natalie, who now saw herself in a position of power. With directing the President-elect to Alora's Dream Haven, she now just needed to check up on her investment.

"Beth, could you call Mrs. Adams?" she said as she brought up her tablet.

The AI responded, "Yes, ma'am. Calling."

Sharron said, "Hello?"

"Hello, Mrs. Adams, this is Natalie from Dimensions. How are you doing?"

Sharron let out a deep yawn. "We just got back, and we're drained. Flying through these different time zones takes a toll on the body."

"I definitely understand. So, how did everything go at Alora's?" asked Natalie.

"It went well. There was a lot of transparency on both ends. We set up a secretive two-week session in early December. Only the people who are pivotal will know. Everything is being done very discreetly, giving my husband almost a full month of recovery."

Sharron had taken a liking to Natalie following their conversation immediately after the meeting last week, where her husband had been told of the grave prophecy.

November 13th, 2024

After the suggestion from Natalie, the head doctor, Eric Atkins, had begun looking into Alora's Dream Haven. The President-elect was in the room, trying to unravel the mystery of what this company was and why this was his first time hearing about it. But Sharron quietly excused herself. This heinous prophetic curse had her emotions all over the place. And Natalie could feel something was going on with the First Lady.

Sharron stepped out of the room, covered her face with her hands, and sped to the women's restroom. Natalie excused herself as well and followed the emotional woman.

Sharron was in the bathroom stall, crying a cry that had fermented inside of her. She thought, at least for a little while, she could sit on the pale porcelain seat and flood out her heart.

"Ms. Adams?" asked Natalie as she entered the bathroom.

Sharron was trying to get her words out, but the guilt started to eat her up alive. "I'm, uh, I'm alright," she said while her emotion began to pour out of her.

Natalie walked up to the stalls and sat in the one next to her. She put her head down and confided in Sharron.

A solemn Natalie said, "When I was in my third year at Dimensions they thrust me into the leadership position. I didn't have any knowledge or experience of running a company, especially one as different as Dimensions. I had no blueprint to follow, no outline, just a hunger to succeed. When all hope was lost, and we were about to close our doors for good, the Zachariah Gross case found its way to us. It was ordained; it's like, it's like God chose Dimensions for that case. Here are two gentlemen who are so blind to the carnage they were unleashing. Carnage that Dimensions would have to sift through. Was it a terrible, terrible case with the most vile and sadistic human beings walking God's green earth? Yes. But that was the most important case in the history of Dimensions."

Sharron took a deep breath and lifted her chin, her eyes narrowing with determination. Her heart, once racing with uncertainty, now steadied as a newfound sense of purpose settled over her like a warm blanket. Her hands, previously trembling, now clenched into fists at her sides, ready to face whatever lay ahead.

Natalie sighed. "So, you see, sometimes devastating, life-changing situations come to bring forth a person's character and greatness. So, the question is, First Lady, what will this situation unlock in you?"

Natalie got up. "It just takes a little bit of faith in yourself."

Then she slowly walked out of the bathroom.

A few moments later, Sharron came out of the restroom and slowly walked up on Natalie as she was about to head back into the room with the President-elect. She stopped and waited for Sharron. She stood right beside Natalie but didn't make eye contact.

Sharron simply said, "Thank you, Natalie. You don't know how much your words helped me. Can I be candid? Parts of me are glad about this horrible prophecy."

She stared ahead; her gaze almost stoic. Sharron continued, "Over the years, I could tell something had changed with Kirk. I don't know – his character, his mannerism, his—his soul. The closer he got to his goals, the more distant he became."

Natalie stared straight ahead, looking at the door the President-elect was behind. "Look at every trial as an opportunity for success and, in the midst of the tribulation, to enhance your character."

Sharron let out a solemn, "Thank you."

Right after the meeting, the First Lady and Natalie exchanged numbers. Natalie would call Sharron and get crucial updates, staying abreast on steps the President-elect was taking.

As busy as Natalie was, she took on people and political engagements as a job. She especially excelled at being involved with people who could take her company to new heights. She could be the most impactful, empathetic, and knowledgeable person someone could have the pleasure of knowing.

However, in the same breath, the foundation of her behavior rested in what she could benefit from the situation. Natalie became a mastermind of the highest hierarchy at the concept of manipulation. Sometimes she was not even aware she was doing it; that was how good she became. Natalie knew how to play the crowd. She was empathic, so she knew exactly what to say to pull on Sharron's heartstrings. It wasn't just about empowering her, but also how this situation could get her closer to her goal.

Present day

In Escondido, San Diego, at Alora's Dream Haven, they were deciding on the team to go into President Adams' dreams.

Dr. Eve; the VP, William Grant; the CFO, Dianna Wellborn; and CLO, Cedrick Clemmons, all walked down the halls of the immaculate building.

"Ladies and gentlemen, our next patient presents an opportunity on a very monumental scale. We need our very best and most seasoned Ubuntu Joiners. I want this to go as flawless as possible. The President-elect will be here in the next two weeks to receive preparation. What is Alora doing to make sure it's successful?" asked Dr. Eve as the four of them headed towards a conference room.

Dianna said, "There are several legal statues that must be ahead too, but we are making sure it is all taken care of. His name at Alora's will be patient F7P9, from here on out. F7P9 will be escorted into gate 128. At eight a.m. on Monday, December second, he will be in contact with only the two Ubuntu Joiners and Dr. Eve.

"Once they have his prep work handled on December fourth, at eleven a.m., they will induce him with Zulu and Dream Walk on his Daraja. Now, what assessments are made will dictate what procedure we perform, the Augmented or the Allurement session."

"Who will be our two Ubuntu Joiners for F7P9?" asked the doctor.

Right on cue, William said, "June Ling," as he ushered them into the conference room.

Everyone sat down and brought their attention to the ninety-inch TV mounted to the wall.

"June Ling is our youngest and most accomplished employee. She has saved 273 patients in a span of seven years. Ms. Ling came into our company at twenty-two and has been rolling ever since. She is always positive, with a very upbeat personality. Definitely a glass-half-full kind of person," said William as he chuckled.

Dr. Eve pulled up June Ling's bio. "What do we know about Ms. Ling?"

The VP commented, "Ling moved here from Korea at the age of six. She had always felt like she was different and, when she turned fifteen, started to embrace it. Ling has never been one to go with the trends or fads. She is undoubtedly a trailblazer; she lives life with no cares or worries. Ling's life is her work; she tries her hardest to save as many lives as she can.

"We have the video footage from her last big case," the VP said, pointing up to the TV.

February 2nd, 2017

"Sorry to call you in, Ms. Ling, but we have a serious problem. Judge Harper moved up Tyrese Rodrick's death sentence. The judge wants to see movement in forty-eight hours, or we lose this case," said the assistant nurse frantically.

"What are his vitals?" June asked as she took off her coat.

"He is asleep in the chair in room three. The Zulu has been administered. Everything that the other Ubuntu have tried hasn't been successful. They can't find what is causing his trauma. None of the suggestions will work, and we can't find anything to hide. It seems like everything we do is a lost cause," said the assistant nurse.

June said, "Nobody is a lost cause! Prep me. If this is our final session, then I'm going to give everything I've got to see it through to the end."

When June drifted into the dreamscape, she found herself in a world that mirrored her own yet possessed an otherworldly allure. Her house, with its bland color scheme and typical layout, seemed to blend seamlessly with the ordinary homes around it. However, there was one element that set her house apart from the rest – a picture of her parents, Wong May Ling and Shing Ling, adorned the walls. It was as if their presence cast a mystical aura over the entire abode.

As June made her way through the house towards the back door, the Dajara, a phenomenal bridge, stretched out before her, its surface bathed in a truculent golden glow. The Dajara subjugated an immaculate finish to its will. Its vibrant hues seemed to dance harmoniously, creating a symphony of colors that felt almost heavenly. It was as if June had stumbled upon the doorsteps of New Jerusalem itself.

Stepping onto the bridge, June felt a powerful connection form between her mind and Tyrese's. The bridge acted as a conduit, enhancing any thoughts or emotions that took precedence in her subconscious. It became clear to June that, for this connection to be effective, her mind needed to be clear and focused – a vital requirement for Tyrese's transformation.

June walked cautiously across the Dajara, letting the process carefully filter her thoughts. It allowed her to be one with Tyrese putting them both on the same neurological frequency. His dream became her dream. With that being the case, why was Tyrese regurgitating all the suggestions?

June walked up to Tyrese as he sulked outside on his porch.

"Doc, they're going to execute me in a month. And you know what, I deserve it," Tyrese uttered in self-loathing.

June picked his head up. "We all make mistakes…"

Tyrese turned away, disgusted. "Go ahead with that crap, Doc. I know what I did. Trying to change my life's, uh, uh, trajectory just might not be in the cards for me. It may be time for some good old-fashioned acceptance and accountability."

June cried out a heartbroken, "I don't buy into that logic. You can be the worst of the worst but still deserve a second chance."

"Doc, what if it was your loved ones I killed, huh?" Tyrese asked with a great deal of remorse. "What if it was your son or daughter whose life I took?"

June said with total confidence, "Then I would want you to spend every waking second trying to redeem yourself. By affecting every life you could for the better."

She extended her hand to help him off the floor.

"Alright, Doc, what do we do now?" Tyrese said as he accepted her hand.

She hurried and walked into Tyrese's house and frantically looked for an object. Something that kept the horrors of his diabolical acts in his mind. In the dream world, they called it a totem.

"We are missing something."

But every piece of furniture, every item, had been accounted for. From the lamp his great-grandmother passed down to his mother before she passed away – that held a very emotionally symbolic moment – to the piece of candy he stole from his uncle and got beaten senseless for.

In the residence of a person's dream, everything in the home had a memory that connected to a totem. And that was how Alora's had the power to specialize in the alteration or transformation of a person's character inside dreams. Alora's took the totems associated with a critical memory and empowered the person to overcome. However, in this case, they were seeing the person totally accepting of the changes, but something was causing him to revert back. A memory. Or it could be something that had positioned itself in the crevice of his soul.

"Give it up, Doc, it's hopeless. I came into this world as a nobody, and that's how I am leaving." Tyrese put his hand by his heart.

June looked at him and then went back to looking for clues. "Is that some kind of oath?"

"Naw, Doc, that's my war wound. When I got initiated in my first gang."

As June continued to look, she said, "Oh, God, please spare me the details."

"Well, Doc, this was my very first robbery for the seventh street crew. I went in with three of the young guys like me, looking to make their name in the drug underworld. It was supposed to be a quick in and out. But as we were leaving with the cash, the owner followed us out the door and let off two shots. I turned. One missed, then the other went through my chest about six centimeters from my heart," said Tyrese as he continued to rub the wound.

June slowly stood up in full awareness and then gave Tyrese her undivided attention.

"The guys I was with took me to the hideout. They patched me up and sent me back out. The bullet is still by my heart," Tyrese said. "It became a reminder that, from that point on, every wrong decision has made me this—this horror of a man you see before you."

June said excitedly, "Wait, so are you telling me that the bullet is still inside you?"

"Yep. I love the looks I get when I go through the metal detectors. Doc, can you imagine a convict on death row causing the metal detectors to go off?" he said as he laughed.

June said, "That's it! That's the answer! The suggestion will not stay because you have a totem that is physically a part of you. Something to remind you of the lives you have taken."

Present Day

They turned from the TV and brought their attention back to William.

"Ms. Ling's perseverance and dedication make her perfect for this opportunity. When they removed the bullet from Mr. Roderick, that's what was causing the therapy to be unsuccessful. Through his transformation, the judge changed his initial sentence and gave Mr. Rodgers more time. So, you see, not only does June hold a person's life in high regard, but she has also shown she has the ability to adapt. A will to keep going when all hope is lost," William said, confident in his selection.

Dr. Eve said, "Let's vote. All in favor? Well, there's no need to vote against."

William said carefully, "Now, our next candidate is Passion Taylor…"

Dianna sighed. Cedrick laughed. Dr. Eve sat quietly.

"So, should we even cue the footage of her greatest success stories?"

Cedrick said, "Who else is on the list?"

"Look, before we had our sights on Ling, it was always Ms. Taylor. She was the company's go-to woman. Passion always got the tough assignments and still managed to come out on top. We asked her to be superwoman when we were still finding our identity as a company. Passion has trained our best Ubuntu and made recommendations that ended up changing this company. She was our lifeline, and now we want to treat her like she didn't have a hand at building this company?" William asked forcefully.

Cedrick responded, "William, I understand what you are saying, but let's not sit here and act like Passion didn't fail on the most important case in Alora's history. The Demario Evans case was supposed to catapult us into the sunset. We had two major – not towns, not cities – but *countries* in our grasp!"

"Calm down, Cedrick," said Dr. Eve.

Cedrick responded with even more aggression, "No, ma'am, the VP needs to hear this. That deal was supposed to usher us into a new age. Not only were we going to be financially secure, but that was going to introduce us to the public. The power of words, sir, making Alora's a household name. Giving us several chapters to operate all around the world. And one minor mistake, one miscalculation that Passion made, sent the whole thing crashing down. Now we have another chance with the President of the United States as our patient, and you're prompting us to put faith in the woman that destroyed it the first time?"

William looked at everybody in the conference room. He put his head down and then spoke. "You are right. I can't fight with your logic. But the President-elect is the most important patient we've ever had at this company. Assuming everything will be a walk in the park, then it doesn't matter who we send in. But what if all hell breaks loose, and they have to operate spur of the moment? Then it is absolutely essential that June and Passion are present. Because if we fail, any way we look at it, we are done. At least we have a much better shot of success with the chosen Ubuntu. You asked me earlier who else we had on the list; this is the list."

Dr. Eve said solemnly, "Votes? Those who are in favor? And those that are against? Three to one. So, we have our two Ubuntu Joiners."

"Dr. Eve, you have an important phone call on line five," the secretary said over the PA system.

"William, finish up here. I'm going to take it in my office," said Dr. Eve.

Dr. Eve walked into her office and picked up the phone. "Hello?"

"Doctor why am I hearing that we have accepted the President-elect as a patient?" asked Senator Carter.

Dr. Eve said sternly, "How do you turn the President of the United States away? You didn't see him crying for our help. I believe we can fix him and return him to normal."

"Dr. Eve, we both know what is in Adams' mind. What do you feel like you can accomplish?"

Dr. Eve pleaded, "I believe we can fix him"

Carter huffed while tapping his finger on the side of the phone. "The risks are too great. There are a million things that could go wrong, but only one thing to go right. If this information comes to light, it's both of our heads on the chopping block. They will find out that I own a hundred percent of Alora's, and not only will we get arrested and be thrown under the prison, everything we've worked for will have an immaculate fall."

Dr. Eve began to grow teary-eyed. She put her head down in disgust. "Senator," she pleaded. "I'm tired. I'm tired of all the lies, all the deceit. I covered up so many secrets. I can't even remember them all anymore. I feel like fixing the President-elect so he can bypass this prophecy can make us righteous again. It can realign our souls, put us back on the right track."

"Please, Eve, don't do this! You'll be fired, and, with the legal ramifications, they will revoke your medical license. If you go through with this, I will have to take matters into my own hands," snarled Carter sinisterly.

Dr. Eve said softly but resolutely, "Senator, you can't run Alora's without me. If you get rid of me, then the entire establishment will come crashing down."

Senator Carter let out a taunt from his very soul. "Just because you serve a purpose doesn't mean you're indispensable."

And then he hung up the phone.

Overture 6 – The Battleground

There is a war going on inside you. It's the forces of God and the forces of the devil. And, since we have free will, the very option to choose, this war is very real. On one aspect, we have God and His undying love, unchanging grace, and unlimited power, and on the other hand is Satan, known as the Prince of the Air. He is willing to give you your desires only if you denounce Jesus the Son. This battleground that I speak of is the battle for our soul. God wants us to have life, to be a beacon of hope, to be a director into the warm embrace of Christ Jesus. But the devil wants us to fail in every way. He wants us to believe Christ has abandoned us, so that we may discourage more souls from coming to Christ.

Which one will you choose?

Marcus Douglas

Chapter 6 – Garnered Two Very Different Souls

November 21st, 2024

Natalie was in her office, and even though she had all the up-to-date information concerning the President-elect, she still felt like she was in the dark. No matter what information she received to stay two steps ahead, she always felt like she was two steps behind.

After the Zachariah Gross case, Natalie had transformed into an incredibly private person, but she had a talent for being meticulous and calculating in her actions. Her strength lay in auditory learning – she could absorb information simply by listening. Even in Natalie's early teens, she discovered that she could hear a song just once and then play it back flawlessly. This sparked the habit of talking to herself as a way to further enhance her skills.

"The pieces are in motion. All I need to do is hope for the most favorable outcome," she said.

Natalie had the folder with the now-seventeen prophecies in front of her. She grew frustrated, and, in the midst of going through prophecies on the President-elect, she slammed closed the folder and threw it on the floor.

"There is more that I could be doing," she said to herself, irritated.

But there was one question Natalie continued to overlook. Through all her elaborate schemes and meticulous planning, there was something that was so simple but even more dire. What if that prophecy was authentic? What if it was something built off the President-elect's passion? It was a spur-of-the-moment decision followed by a series of cascade failures. *But how?* She wondered. *The President has to have Republican and Democratic backing alike. Even if he was somehow secretly a mass murderer, he couldn't institute any laws without Congress approval.* Natalie's mind raced desperately to put the pieces together.

In the midst of her thoughts, Natalie turned her head sideways, and, at the bottom of the security cabinet, she saw a large brown envelope; she reached down to get it.

"How did I not see this? It's been years that this has been down here."

She opened the envelope up. "Let's see what we got here." Natalie let out a sigh.

It was from their mentor, Brenden McDowell. He had documented a dream. It concerned a man who would be President. He said this man would single-handedly start wars and bring utter destruction across the globe. The document listed the date as…"

Natalie turned the paper back and forth as she softly asked, "That's it?"

"We followed Adams for months in 2019, 2020, and 2022, and there was not a bit of criminal activity."

Natalie sat up attentively in her chair. She slowly thought of Brenden. Then a daydream took precedence of her thoughts. Natalie smirked about Brenden, whom she used to be madly in love with. It was like the key to her heart was opened by the name Brenden McDowell. Natalie broke out of her trance and studied the cryptic note that was very intriguing, to say the least.

But I need to get more information.

Natalie jumped on her tablet and started searching for Brenden. She knew he was titled by the Christian religion as a prophet at a church organization called Pillar of Hope. That was not foreign to her because Brenden had always been a leader. She vaguely remembered that Brenden's mother was deep in the church. But that was so long ago. Natalie went on the church's website and was trying to set up a meeting with him, but his books were filled until the middle of next year. So, she decided to meet with one of the deacons.

Natalie had little time. At least this would allow her to get her foot into the door. Her meeting was today at four p.m.

She tapped her nails against the desk. Going to attempt to see Prophet McDowell, after everything that happened in the past…

But she needed to make sure that she had every variable in order to complete her objective. Seeing her ex-fiancé was inevitable.

Natalie jumped up and put an "out of the office" sign on her door. She said into her phone, "Beth, can you bring the car around?"

"Yes, Ms. Massey," said the AI.

The car pulled up, and the suicide doors opened as Natalie stepped in the car.

"Ready," Natalie exclaimed.

The doors closed.

Beth asked, "Where to, Ms. Massey?"

"The Pillar of Hope headquarters in Charlottesville, Virginia."

As the car pulled off, Beth said, "Uploading directions, it is approximately three hours and forty-seven minutes. Would you like some music to keep you entertained?"

"No, play me anything on the internet that you have on Prophet Brenden McDowell," Natalie said as she got comfortable and put her feet up in total relaxation.

"Yes, ma'am, playing."

"Twelve years ago, before he was the Prophet Brenden McDowell, he started the psychic group known as Dimensions and made leaps and bounds with the company. But, ten years ago, he had a vision from God, which caused him to step down from a very promising career. Not knowing which way to turn, his life was at a standstill."

The video continued to play as Natalie's blinks started to get heavier and heavier.

"It wasn't until he went to a church service that he began the path God had him on. Brenden started preaching and teaching the Word of God, prophesying toward all walks a life all over the globe. Brenden has become the presiding prelate of a wonderful establishment called Pillar of Hope, Inc. in Charlottesville, Virgínia, acting as the head of 129 ministries all over the world."

The words become distorted as Natalie fell asleep and dreamt of the past.

March 13, 2013

Brenden confidently said, "We have been making progress in baby steps. When the case of the North Carolina bombing was taking place, Dimensions was fighting and clamoring for a seat with law enforcement. I mean, there are lives in the balance, and we are battling for the legitimacy of Dimensions' authenticity. And Dimensions is not without a lack of understanding – we know there's a lot of legalities that are at the height of the foundation of the law. We are the…"

"Cut, cut, cut, surely, we can find someone else. I mean, these guys are a joke," said the head reporter as the crew got their equipment and walked off.

"Freaks, what were their names? Detention?" They all laughed as they got in their news van.

Natalie stepped closer to Brenden and said, her demeanor full of excitement, "It's like you said, sir, people fear what they don't understand."

"Yes, Natalie. But Dimensions will be such a well-oiled machine that they'll be clawing at us for our help," said Brenden.

Dominique and Monique responded together, "That's right."

Donnie asked, "What do we do now, sir?"

"We are going to show perseverance." Brenden had a thought. "You know, what we need is familiarity. Yeah, yeah, a branch of our organization that are special but still very much human."

Natalie was in awe of Brenden's commitment and dedication. He had been their mentor for about a year, and she was taken aback by Brenden's confidence. Everything he excelled at she found herself not only lacking but longing for. But moreover, under professionalism, Natalie found herself falling for him as Brenden continued to hone in on the craft of Dimensions.

She envisioned them taking romantic strolls in the park, or a lovely picnic. Natalie would be sitting on a cool, bright lime-green beach towel with little specks of burnt orange while Brenden took out all the food in the picnic basket that enticed Natalie's pallet. An array of half-sliced ham and honey turkey sandwiches, potato chips, grapes, and cherries.

The exciting cascade was enchanted with wine glasses that garnered the selections of a white peach tea or a sangria sparkling cider. It was capped off with a delicious dessert of simple-but-elegant chocolate-covered strawberries that Brenden would feed Natalie.

The smell of love radiated its dominance in the air. Brenden sealed the rendezvous with a magical kiss and whispered, "I love you."

Out of nowhere, the skies abruptly darkened. It looked like the heavens were about to open the floodgates, but it was far from it. The sky jolted from a warm, sunny, vibrant orange and yellow to a dark blue and murky smoked gray. The lively grass instantly withered away into its dead alter-ego self. The random people who walked aimlessly through the park were zombie-like corpses, and their pets were all mutated. The dogs and cats had dead skin, dried open lesions, and maggots that tore through their open flesh.

A figure in a black robe and a Guy Fawkes mask appeared, their voice distorted and mechanical. As the anonymous figure walked deliberately towards Brenden and Natalie, Brenden stood in front of Natalie like a protective shield.

The mysterious figure asked, "Do you know who I am?"

Brenden yelled, "Natalie, get behind me! You will never manipulate or overtake us!"

The figure let out this diabolical laugh, like a war cry. "Brenden, you fool! I already have."

The individual in the black robe waved his hand at Brenden and immediately threw him back. It was like a person successfully swatting a fly. The masked figure put their thumb on Natalie's forehead and let out an eerie, "Remember… The horrors, I am the Morning Star."

As the echo of the figure's voice faded into the abyss, Natalie felt a shiver of raw terror race down her spine. The world seemed to stretch and warp in front of her eyes, reality distorting as she stared into the depths of nothingness.

A series of grotesque images flashed before her: burning buildings, torn bodies, a sea of blood. She saw Zachariah Gross, his cold eyes devoid of all humanity, methodically committing his heinous acts. Her mind fell victim to the horrors, but there was no escaping them. The memories were not her own, yet they were seared into her psyche.

Zachariah, a man of both humbleness and stature, cast an imposing shadow over the narrow streets of Martinsburg, Maryland. When Zachariah was first caught, it put the small town on the front page of every broadcast news channel. The town's secrets were unveiled, the mysteries of this unearthly evil exposed. Though his pleasant appearance and his bubbly outlook on life made it effortless to hide in plain sight, Zachariah's face and sparkling, baby-blue eyes were easy to get captivated by. His unmistakable softness in his demeanor made him a beloved figure among the townsfolk.

His roles within the community varied as much as they were numerous. He often moonlighted as the town's clerk, at a restaurant called Soul Mood. As the sun began its retreat towards twilight, Zachariah would smoothly transition into his role as a volunteer firefighter, ensuring each home carried a light brighter than any threat of darkness. But it was in his role as a teacher at the local Sunday school where he truly found his calling.

"I am the Prince of Darkness," Lucifer's voice echoed in Natalie's head.

Zachariah sat by an oak tree on Sunday mornings and told Bible stories. His deep, rumbling voice would travel through the park during these story sessions, captivating not just the children but also any adult who passed by. As laughter echoed through the air and curious eyes gleamed with interest, Zachariah found happiness within these fragments of shared joy.

"Good morning, young ones!" Zachariah garnered a warm smile, his eyes twinkling with kindness as the children gathered around him. "Today, I shall tell you a tale of bravery and trusting in God, the story of David and Goliath.

"Once upon a time, there was a shepherd boy named David who lived in Israel and took care of his family's sheep.

"David's father, Jesse, asked him to bring food to his brothers, who were soldiers in the army of Israel, fighting against the Philistines. When David arrived at the camp, he could hear their enemy, Goliath, taunting and insulting the Israelites. This giant of a man challenged them to send a soldier to fight him one-on-one. While all the soldiers were too afraid to face Goliath, young David was brave and willing to help his people.

"He asked King Saul for permission to fight Goliath and eventually received it, despite the king's concerns for his safety. Rather than using the armor and weapons offered by the king, David chose to use only a sling and five smooth stones. Goliath mocked David as he approached with no traditional weapons, but David confidently declared that he came in the name of God. With a single stone from his sling, David struck Goliath in the forehead, killing him instantly. The Philistines were terrified and fled while the Israelites chased them across the battlefield. David's bravery and, most of all, faith made him famous throughout Israel, and he was seen as a hero. Eventually, he became their king."

Excited whispers filled the air as the children settled in closer, their eyes wide with anticipation.

"Was David scared, Mister Zachariah?" a little girl with pigtails asked, her voice filled with wonder.

Zachariah chuckled softly before replying, "Oh no, ma'am, David was confident. He knew that if God is for him, then who could be against him?" He paused for effect, letting the suspense linger.

As the story unfolded, the children gasped at David's daring feat and cheered when he triumphed over Goliath. Zachariah's voice carried them through a journey of courage and belief, weaving lessons of faith and inner strength into the fabric of their young minds.

It was time to go back inside as Zachariah said, "Remember, my little Davids," as his eyes became one with the young audience, "No matter how small you may feel, your heart can hold immeasurable bravery and perseverance."

Zachariah told these immaculate and uplifting stories. It was like there were two versions of Zachariah; on one hand, he yearned for the innocence he lost many years ago. He felt an uncanny need to empower the children with valor and perseverance. He wanted to save them from the hunger that was embedded in him by his father but perfected by his mother. And on the other, Zachariah had a very terrifying and deprived thirst that, by normal means, could not be quenched.

He wanted the kids to have faith, strength and wisdom, so they could face those challenges of the world and show bravery when confronted with their own David situation. The catch was that he was the Goliath he spoke so ill about. *The hunger gnawed at him, a relentless whisper in his mind. He clenched his fists, fighting against the urge that had become both his curse and his comfort.* It was almost like Zachariah garnered two very different souls.

Zachariah would use these narratives to prey on these young minds' innocence – crafting morals and virtues into each tale's fabric. From Joesph's dreams, Job's triumph, Moses and the parting of the Red Sea, to the birth of Jesus Christ – each story carried a lesson, a prayer for their innocent hearts to grow good and wholesome;

nevertheless, a diabolic craving for each one of the young one's souls he prayed for lurked. What a broken and depraved man he was, but due to his mom's excellent sculpting, you would never know.

"I am like a roaring lion," Lucifer's war cry played in Natalie's thoughts.

Zachariah was frantic. Although it was his fourth time doing this unspeakable crime, it still got his adrenaline pumping. The thrill of potentially getting caught was like fire in his veins. His mind was being pulled in thirty different directions like previous times. However, he was poised and calculating. Zachariah played back in his mind how he had just taken one of the most well-known politicians, Kody Perkins's, son. Kaleb was a Caucasian child-actor-turned-star. He was known for his roles in the critically acclaimed musical, *Sugar Pie, Honey Bun* and played in *Star of the Ages*. At the height of his powers, Kaleb, at six-years old, was the youngest to be nominated for an Oscar. This child was well known all around the world.

He glanced at the rearview mirror again, checking on Kaleb's unconscious form slumped in the back seat. "I can't believe that I got you," Zachariah muttered darkly at the reflection of Kaleb's peaceful face while he twisted the wheel to navigate the winding roads leading to the cabin in the woods.

The car rode along the rough terrain, but Zachariah barely noticed as he recited his plan repeatedly in his head. He knew he had to work quickly; the chloroform would only last so long before Kaleb woke up again—but something deep inside told him he couldn't afford any slip-ups this time around.

Lucifer, the diabolical fiend, deliberately found Zachariah. It was after his second kidnapping and murder, and Zachariah could feel a heavy weight on his conscience. As Lucifer whispered detailed accounts of his last killing in his ear, Zachariah's heart raced with fear. He thought he was caught for sure this time. But to his surprise, Lucifer had other plans. Lucifer wanted to enhance Zachariah's crimes, upstaging even his previous dramatic murders.

That would turn Zachariah into an even more proficient killer. From that day on, they joined forces and worked together to create a reign of terror unlike any other. The night seemed to grow darker around them as they plotted and schemed, becoming a dynamic duo that struck fear into the souls of all who crossed their paths.

At last, reaching his destination, an old cabin nestled deep within the trees, Zachariah stepped out of the car to survey his surroundings. He dragged Kaleb's limp body from the back seat and hoisted him over his shoulder with a grunt before heading towards the cabin doors.

As he entered the dimly lit space, Zachariah set Kaleb down carefully on a nearby bed and bound his hands and feet with rough rope he found inside the cabin—just for good measure, should Kaleb wake before he had a chance to administer another dose of chloroform later during his captivity here at Zachariah's personal prison made especially for Kaleb Perkins.

Lucifer's schemes and plans had worked beautifully. Being in the exact time, at the designated place, allowed him to grab and subdue Kaleb. Zachariah gave a satisfied nod at Lucifer's plan and his handiwork to secure Kaleb safely against any potential premature escape attempts from Kaleb.

Lucifer yelled, "I am Lucifer, and I am here!"

Overture 7 – Soul Mate, Part 1

What is a soul mate? By definition, it is a person with whom one feels a deep or natural affinity. This affinity may involve similarity, romantic love, sexual activity, spirituality, and trust. The term comes from Buddhism and Hinduism, but the expression was adopted in the mid-1900s by all other walks of life.

When you see these words, they are basically a deep connection or a natural oneness another individual has on their counterpart. But having somebody who is exactly like you may not always be the best thing. Diamonds are made through pressure. Metal sharpens metal; there has to be a tug in the alternate direction for growth to occur. And if that is the case, what really is a soul mate?

While the idea of soulmates often leans toward romance, my own experience with the concept was entirely different. About thirty years ago, I was in high school with my younger sister. The school did this compatibility test, a 100-question quiz they entered in a database, trying to find out who in the school was the greatest match. My younger sister and I ended up ninety-eight percent compatible, the highest average in the school. Does that mean my sister and I were soul mates? I think we carried a lot of similarities, but we were also greatly influenced by our mother. So, it is understandable why we matched so well.

Have you ever had someone you considered your soul mate?

Marcus Douglas

Chapter 7 – *Merged With Their Son's Soul*

Present Day, November 21st, 2024

"Ms. Massey, we are here," said Beth.

As Natalie jolted awake, the clips on Brenden were still playing.

"You will be a mighty woman of God, you will command greatness in every aspect, and you will never be like your father," spoke a stern prophet McDowell.

The video showed the woman in an emotional state after that prophecy.

The prophet continued, "Ah yes, because you share a lot of similarities with your dad, you fear that your destinies will be intertwined. But God wants to let you know that is not the case. There is power in your perseverance. It's not about you holding on, but about you letting go."

Natalie was fully awake, and although her meeting wasn't for another hour, she was somewhat curious about the amount of success Brenden had attained.

"I'm ready," Natalie said, and once again, the suicide doors opened.

Pillar of Hope was a testament to human ingenuity and artistic brilliance. The church's Romanesque-Byzantine style exuded grandeur, with statues of saints on the exterior and finely crafted mosaics inside. Byzantine influence could be seen in the masterful use of mosaic and marble. Behind the church was the headquarters building, where day-to-day operations were conducted with utmost precision.

Natalie stepped out of the car, marveling at Brenden's journey. Ten years ago, he had left Dimensions. Now, he led 129 churches as the head diocese.

Natalie walked towards the entrance, only to be met by an altercation. There were eleven men and women with picket signs saying things like, 'The end is coming; get your house in order,' but the one that really caught her attention was, 'The President is the anti-Christ.'

Natalie was taken aback. She was frightened at the thought that others knew of the prophecy.

The deacons of Pillar of Hope were trying to convince the protesters that they didn't engage in politics.

The head of the protesters, Benard Stacy, said, "The Good Shepherd teaches us that you can't be of this natural world and not be a part of politics. Our entire existence has a political foundation."

The lead deacon, Mark Halloway, said, "The Bible says, 'And be not conformed to this world: but be ye transformed by the renewing of your mind.' So, you see, my good sir, we have to be above the standards of this world."

"And I agree, but how do we connect with them if we are both untethered? We can't be too spiritual where we are not any earthly good and too earthly where we are not any spiritually good," spoke a solemn Benard.

Mark said earnestly, "My good sir, the prophet teaches us we have to be a beacon of light, a pillar of hope. We must be steadfast and unmovable. When we are needed, they know where to find us."

"But what about those people who don't have the means to get to you? What about those people down and out? Who need God's loving embrace but don't know where to start? They just need to see God's love is willing to come and rescue them, especially with the evil that's about to be unleashed." Benard's heartfelt word was met with emotions.

"Sir, evil has been in the world since the beginning of time. Prophet McDowell teaches us…"

"If your prophet is so efficient at prophecy, why is it that he can't see this diabolic evil coming? We have linked up with other true believers around the country to prepare. If you are not going to listen, at least you owe it to your saints for the truth," Benard interrupted.

While Benard and Mark went back and forth, Natalie walked up to one of the protesters and asked, "What is your organization's name?"

"We are called the Peculiar People," said a woman named Me Me.

Natalie asked, "How do I join or be a part?"

Me Me gave Natalie a pamphlet. "We are meeting tonight at the old Renaissance Building at the corner of Franklin Road and Myer Street. Now, this might sound strange, but we come masked. I know it's weird, but some people hold key positions in the political scheme. They believe in what the Good Shepherd is saying. It gives everybody—"

Natalie interrupted, "No need to explain, I get it. It provides protection for all those involved."

"Why, yes, that's exactly it," responded Me Me.

As Natalie continued to walk past the protesters, she made it through the entrance. At the desk was a secretary named Daphné.

As Natalie approached, Daphné said, "I'm so sorry, these people, the Peculiar People." She scoffed at the thought. "Ever since President Adams got elected, they've been coming around more frequently. They've been requesting persistently to see our presiding Prophet McDowell. This, this Good Shepherd would not hold a flame to Prophet McDowell. I have physically seen him dismantle charlatans like this person before."

"I'm just playing devil's advocate, but what if what Good Shepherd says is true?" asked Natalie.

Daphné gave an intense response as if she was offended by the sheer notion of the question. "Their entire organization is talking recklessly about our President. If it was something that serious, I'm sure our prophet would have told us already."

But Natalie remained quiet because she knew that Brenden had the first prophecy about the President-elect. Not only making bold predictions about Adams but making the same exact claims as his nemesis.

Natalie shifted the conversation. "Hey, I have a meeting with a deacon Halloway in about forty-five minutes."

"Oh, yes, you just walked past him, I'm so, so sorry; excuse my ranting. What is your name?" asked Daphné.

"Natalie Massey, the…"

"Head of Dimensions of America. Oh my God! It's really you." Daphné came from around the desk and gave Natalie the biggest hug and started to weep. "My daughter and nephew were in the schools that those bombers were going to attack, but, thanks to your organization—it was, was, you saved my family, the salvation to my future," Daphné said as her crying intensified.

Natalie drew into the warm embrace of the gesture as Daphné started to shake in spite of her happiness. Natalie sat her down in her chair behind the desk and said, "You are welcome."

Daphné exclaimed, "If there is anything I can do, I will be honored to oblige."

"Well, do you think I can have a quick sit-down today with Prophet McDowell?" asked Natalie.

Daphné tore a piece of paper and started to write on it as she let out a sorrowful, "Oh, I apologize, Natalie, but the prophet is super busy. His schedule doesn't open up until the end of April. But you already have a meeting with the chairperson of the deacon board. You can wait, or we can reschedule?" Daphné said as she slid the paper that she had written, "Prophet McDowell is on an emergency sabbatical."

—

At the same time, President Adams was telling his parents of the grave prophetic curse.

"…and the prophecy predicts that I will be the world's most infamous mass murderer," the President-elect said as he softly wept.

"Dad, Mom… I, I just don't know what to do. Ever since I was a young child, I was always confident in my life's direction." Adams cried harder. "But now, I'm lost. I have no clue which way I need to go."

"No, no, no, this can't be true," Helena cried as she got up to console her son.

Stanely got up and walked, agitated, toward the door and stopped put his head down and asked, "Son, do you trust Dimensions?"

"Dad, I swear, I don't want to believe it. But something's changing in me. Sharron sees it too. The anger, it's like a fire under my skin. I try to push it down, but it's growing. It's like once this prophecy was revealed to me, I am getting so impatient, and extremely emotional." Adams let out a sea full of tears.

"I would never think in a million years that this prophecy would be true, but now, I don't know what to think," Adams added as he put his head down, returning to his mother's embrace.

Stanely closed his eyes, trying to fight the emotion that was battling to matriculate to the surface. His heart merged with his son's soul.

Stanley walked over and kneeled in front of his son as Adams cried immensely. He whispered, trying to hold in his tears, "Hey, listen to this, when you were four years old, I was spraying pesticide for rodents. I had gone to the hardware store and brought some home.

"It was concentrated, so I had to dilute it. I took a cup and poured the pesticide in it. And then filled the container. I went out and was spraying where I knew we normally get mice, and I didn't think about it.

"An hour later, I went back inside to find the glass cup of pesticide half gone. I looked all over for the evidence; I even asked your mom. But then we saw you passed out on the floor and automatically assumed the worst. We rushed you to the hospital. The doctors couldn't pump your stomach because it was a liquid. You started to spike a fever, and, because the poison was still in your body, nothing they gave you lowered your temperature."

Stanely got on both knees to make eye contact with his son. "The doctors gave you this black liquid chalk substance to make you throw up, but that didn't work. Your body started to fail, and you went in and out of cardiac arrest. The doctor wanted us to get prepared for the worst, and, in the midst of dying and coming back, you asked for a cup of water and threw up the poison." Stanely started to cry.

Adams asked, "Is that why you call me miracle?"

Helena nodded her head with tears in her eyes as she increased the intensity with which she held her son. She whispered a faint, "You should have died that day. But God saw fit that you would survive."

Stanely said, "Not God, but fate. Fate has you sitting before us now. Fate has the final say-so, no prophecy or prophets."

"Okay, Dad, we get it," Adams said as he and Helena giggled through their tears.

Stanely said, "What, oh." He giggled. "I'm just saying that a person can't control what fate says; you can only control yourself. Son, it's about what you believe about you that will be the deciding factor."

They all sat in a brief silence at the echo of those words.

Stanely said as he tapped his son on the leg, "I know what will improve our moods. How about I go into the cellar and get a vintage 1924 chardonnay? What do you say?"

Adams forced a smile through the pain and nodded.

Stanely looked at Helena with a bubbling excitement, and she let out an emotional, "Sure."

Stanely went to the cellar to get the wine.

"Has Dad always been like that, not believing in God?" Adams looked up and asked his mother as she released her embrace.

Helena wiped tears from her eyes. "You know, now that you ask, no. He used to be a strong believer in God. But after you went to the ER for drinking that pesticide, Stanely has never been the same."

"But, Mom, everything about that situation should have killed me. But I'm alive and well; shouldn't that have drawn Dad closer to God, rather than away?"

Helena looked at her son. "You know what, son, I just don't know."

———

Later that night, Natalie went to where the Peculiar People were meeting.

Natalie found the Renaissance Building, an old building that had a lot of wear and tear. About five centuries of no maintenance, no upgrades or enhancements. However, in its heyday, during the 1950s to 1970s, it served as a multi-media concert center, drawing crowds of up to 3000 people. A true visionary marvel, this venue seamlessly transformed from a dazzling concert hall that hosted legendary entertainers like Dean Martin, Bob Dylan, Ray Charles, and James Brown, to an exquisite art museum showcasing the masterpieces of Jacob Lawrence and Sam Gilliam.

Amidst its elegant walls, the glorious alteration allowed it to be a theater. Some of the most popular stage plays took center stage, enchanting audiences with classics like *Fiddler on the Roof* and *Oliver*. However, tragedy struck when the building's owner, Chris Edward III, passed away abruptly from heart failure. He had created a place that prompted love, happiness, and peace, but with his unexpected death, built only hate, sadness, and turmoil. It left his four children scrambling for power and control over their father's legacy. With five decades of dormancy taking its toll, the building was eventually purchased by the Peculiar People at a fraction of its true value.

The massive building was normally at full capacity. However, this was a weekday, where it had a smaller crowd, but still a very intimate setting.

Natalie, wearing a plain white mask, walked through the door. She was intrigued but also frightened. Her mind raced. What all did the Good Shepherd know? What vision was he privileged to? Most importantly, how did that change the landscape of all the people he led?

An older, very well-dressed gentleman came to the podium on the stage. Natalie noticed he had on a formal three-piece suit and expensive cufflinks, and, although he walked with a cane, Natalie could tell he was an influential figure in the organization.

The man said, "Praise the Lord, everybody."

Everyone said, "Praise the Lord."

"Come on, we can do better than that! Praise the Lord, everybody," the man said, increasing his intensity.

Everybody matched the man's passion. "Praise the Lord."

"Amen. I'm known as Abraham; thank you all for coming. We don't think it is a coincidence that you have gathered with us tonight. We don't believe in luck or happenstance; we are not proponents of chance, nor are we students of causality. No, if you are here, it was because you were purposed here. This, ladies and gentlemen, is your destiny. The Word of God mentions throughout the Bible the last days. Look at the person next to you and say to them, 'The last days."

Everybody looked at one another and said, "The last days."

Abraham continued, "In the book of Revelation, God forewarned believers of the events that will unfold in the future. And now, we are witnessing these prophecies come to life before our very eyes. Wars and diseases run rampant; lawlessness pervades society…" Abraham's voice cracked with emotion as he wiped his eyes. "It all comes down to a lack of love for one another." Murmurs of agreement rippled through the crowd. Some nodded solemnly, others exchanged knowing glances.

"It's no wonder that the greatest commandment in the Bible is to love thy neighbor as thyself. But as crucial as it is to work on our love for others, there is an even greater threat we must face. He is mentioned throughout the Bible: in Daniel, chapters seven, eight, and nine; Second Thessalonians, chapter two; Matthew, chapter twenty-four; and all throughout the book of Revelation. He goes by many names but is known as the diabolical anti-Christ."

"We must prepare for the great tribulation. We must put things in place to protect peace on the earth. Not only for the believer's sake but, most importantly, the non-believer. Look at your neighbor and say, 'Love thy brother as thyself,'" said Abraham.

There was a brief silence, and Abraham whispered a faint, "Love thy brother as thyself."

"Without further ado, I bring to the stage the honorable Good Shepherd."

Everybody clapped.

The spotlight illuminated the figure slowly ascending the stage steps. The Good Shepherd looked at his audience through his mask. His appearance was that of a man who inherited knowledge before his time. Natalie couldn't put her finger on it, but, even from her view, his eyes looked God-awfully familiar.

He raised his hand to silence the applause and took his place behind the podium. His voice carried a peaceful tone as he began to speak. "Thank you, Abraham, for your powerful words."

The Good Shepherd continued, "We are indeed living in a time of escalating crisis. Not only are there strict and strenuous attacks on the church, but a very dangerous onslaught to the fabric of truth. Why is this important, you ask? If people want to be delusional, then let them be delusional." The Good Shepherd chuckled as he wiped the corners of his mouth with his handkerchief.

"Do you remember when you were a little kid? And your parents used to teach you that Santa Claus was real? He is making a list, checking it twice, gonna find who is naughty or nice. Some of you were bad and still got gifts!"

Everybody in the audience laughed.

"But as you got older, the world introduced you to paying bills and working a nine to five," the Good Shepherd said comically. "Where is that jolly old fat guy, now that you have responsibilities? The Bible says in First Corinthians, chapter thirteen, 'When I was a child, I talked like a child, I thought like a child, I reasoned like a child. When I became a man, I put childlike things away.' The people of this world have traded their reality for imagination. In their imagination, it allows people to act out their fantasy. And then fantasy becomes laws, and laws become judgments. What the Bible says transforms into hate crimes. With veracity no longer being at the forefront, it is the open gate which the anti-Christ will come through," the Good Shepherd said with all sincerity.

There was utter silence in the room; only his voice echoed through the hall.

"We've been forewarned about these times by our Lord. He has given us His Word as a roadmap for navigating these turbulent days. And if we hold true to it, we will come out the other end stronger and full of hope."

The Good Shepherd continued, "The anti-Christ's ascension is very much real, and he is among us. Readying his position, he hasn't yet been unleashed on this world. That's why it is prudent for us to prepare. This world needs the Peculiar People more than they know. His reign signifies not our defeat, but an opportunity for us to rise above. To stand together and prepare against the darkness encircling us."

As the Good Shepherd spoke, a light slightly blurred his vision. It was a very distinct charm coming from Natalie's necklace. It was a twenty-four-karat white diamond rope but, attached to it, was an engagement ring. The ring would glimmer and shine under the halogen lights. It wasn't distracting, but nonetheless, very noticeable.

The Good Shepherd's gaze lingered on the ring, and, though his voice never wavered, his eyes betrayed a momentary flicker of surprise. "We must remember," he said, shifting his focus back to the congregation, "that it is in our unity that we shall find our strength. Each one of us possesses unique gifts and talents – gems, if you will – that can be used to protect and uplift our community."

The Good Shepherd cleared his throat and continued speaking with renewed vigor. "It is time for us to rise above fear and clothe ourselves in faith. For too long, we have ignored the prophecy of this threat. But no more! I say unto you today, let us take up our shields of faith, put on the full armor of God, and be ready for battle."

A sense of unity washed over the room as heads nodded in agreement, and murmurs of affirmation echoed around them. The Good Shepherd's words were like an ointment to their broken hearts.

As the meeting drew to a close, prayers were said aloud, and people slowly congregated with one another. Many of the crowd wanted to meet the Good Shepherd.

Natalie calmly combed her way to the audience to meet him. When she finally got into his vicinity, she said, "Good Shepherd, your message was insightful, and very invigorating."

"To God be the glory, I'm just a vessel," the Good Shepherd said as he acknowledged the surrounding people, not giving Natalie his full attention.

Natalie's voice cut through the murmuring crowd like a knife. "But, sir, I noticed in your sermon you didn't say anything about President Adams being the anti-Christ."

The room fell deathly silent. It was as if time itself had paused. Abraham's eyes darkened, and with a sharp snap of his fingers, security moved quickly and precise. Their eyes locked onto Natalie, their intent clear.

The Good Shepherd, however, held up a hand to halt security, as his gaze fixed on her. But it wasn't her words that unsettled him, it was the ring like charm around her neck.

The Good Shepherd said, "Ma'am, I'm sure this is a conversation we can have in my office."

Natalie looked around through her mask, and when she saw security surrounding her, she said, "Yes, I will go."

Abraham escorted her to the Good Shepherd's office.

He unlocked the door and ushered her in before closing the door.

Natalie entered the office, a spacious and sophisticated space with off-white walls, chocolate-brown carpeting, and crystal chandeliers. The desk, made from rich redwood, displayed intricate patterns. In the corner were white masks and a casual collection of weathered construction gear, including boots resting beneath the sofa.

The Good Shepherd came through the door and methodically walked slowly around Natalie, looking her up and down again. He placed his Bible on the desk.

"Kirklin Johnson Adams is the anti-Christ." He hovered over his seat, then sat. "I first had the vision long ago."

Overture 8 – Will

Your will is fairly important because it comprises the notion to fight or flight. Will takes everything that the mind and emotions have and combines it into an elixir called desire. Now, will, in my eyes, is the closest characteristic that embodies the soul. It creates action. Even your emotions, to some extent, need your will. My will carries me to consistently write these books. A person taking medicine or working out, or simply getting up for work, requires a vast amount of will. Sometimes your will keeps your actions from what your heart yearns to do, even restraining from the emotional pull of your feelings. How do you measure the strength of your will?

Marcus Douglas

Chapter 8 – Unshackle the Restraints on His Soul

Natalie giggled. "That is a mighty strong accusation to imply about his character."

"Ma'am, that's what visions reveal, the content of a person's character – or their future actions – that they are oblivious toward. That is prophecy, changing somebody's present by God giving you glimpses into a person's future to help mold their life. They become a part of you and you them," said the Good Shepherd.

Natalie said, "You speak as if you have experience with visions."

"I have more experience than you, ma'am," said a confident Good Shepherd.

Natalie scoffed, "You have more experience than me? Please. You have no idea who I am. If you did, you wouldn't be making such preposterous claims."

"A young woman who got her first vision at the age of sixteen. You thought they were hallucinations, until the things you had envisioned started to come true. Then you thought isolation was the key," said the Good Shepherd.

As Natalie looked up at the Good Shepherd speechless, she tried to mask her shock, but with every word he spoke drained the air from the room.

The Good Shepherd continued, "It wasn't until you saw an ad in the newspaper that mentioned looking for people who constantly see or experience paranormal activities. You read that and cried because, for a while, you thought you were the only one. When you made it to your first meet and greet, you hugged the twins so tightly, saying that you finally found your sense of belonging, you found…"

"Purpose," Natalie said as she let out a tear.

"Only select people know that story. You, you truly are…"

The Good Shepherd stood up, walked swiftly toward her, and took off his mask revealing himself to be Brenden McDowell. "Hey ya, Nat."

Natalie took her mask off as well. Butterflies with a mix of confusion started to overtake her. She sensed something in his eyes, but she had no clue that it was her ex-fiancé. She fumbled over her words, "Why, but you, can I, how, how is this possible?"

"Well, about ten years ago—"

Natalie interrupted, "I mean, why? The Good Shepherd and the prophet?"

Brenden began his tale, his voice echoing with regret. "When I left Dimensions, I was lost, unclear in my direction," he began. "My mother, rest in peace, kept constantly inviting me to church. She said, 'You're stepping down from that abomination of an establishment is the best thing that could off happen to you.' So, finally, I went to a church called Revive, and I will never forget it. The pastor spoke life into me that day. A vision came to me; it was as clear as the midday sun yet as elusive as the morning mist."

They sat on the sofa as Brenden continued his story.

"So, everything in my life started to unfold after you, well, we were…"

Natalie slightly put her head down in shame. Brenden tried to force out the words but continued.

"I struggled at first, but like David and his skillful harp playing, my gifts started to make room for me. I started to be the face of Pillar of Hope. And then other churches started to join, and Pillar of Hope wanted me to be their presiding prelate. It's similar to a president, but everything still works by a committee," said Brenden.

"I started to thrive and build the mass body collectively. But God spoke to me and said that He wanted me to break away from Pillar of Hope and start preparing the people for the coming of the anti-Christ. And when I thought I was done with President Adams being the anti-Christ, my ascension in the church was just to prepare me for the heinous prophecy. So, I did what God said, mostly, but I didn't turn away from Pillar of Hope. I stayed and served."

Brenden stood up, disgusted with himself. "I started this faction called the Peculiar People, and I went by the Good Shepherd. Droves of people started to come. It took off immediately. It was the masks, nobody knowing your ethnicity, race, financial status, or political stance."

Brenden was beside himself. Nobody knew his secret; nevertheless, he freely opened his heart to Natalie. It was like the weights that wore his body down started to loosen with every word spoken.

Brenden walked over to his desk while Natalie continued to sit on the sofa. Brenden's thoughts were all over the place. It was like Natalie had been sent there so Brenden could unshackle the restraints on his soul. Brenden picked up his Bible.

"You know, there's a testament in the Word of God about Abraham and Sarah. The Bible states that they were commanded by God to leave their home and travel to a new land that would one day belong to their descendants. God promised to bless and make them into a great nation. Following God's instructions, Abraham brought his wife Sarah, his nephew Lot, and their belongings, and journeyed to Canaan. Ten years later, the couple was still without children. Sarah suggested that Abraham have a child with her servant Hagar from Egypt, and he agreed. This caused tension between Sarah and Hagar, as Sarah felt that Hagar no longer respected her as an authority figure. Hagar fled but returned after being visited by angels. She then gave birth to Ishmael, Abraham's son.

"Later, three men arrived at Abraham and Sarah's tent, and one revealed that Sarah would become pregnant with a son in a year's time. When Sarah overheard this, she laughed to herself at the thought of having a child at her age. However, she did indeed become pregnant and gave birth, just as had been predicted. At the age of one hundred, Abraham named his newborn son Isaac." Brenden's stoic gaze was eerie.

Natalie asked, "I'm sorry, Brenden, but I'm lost on what that has to do with anything."

Brenden walked back over to Natalie. "Don't you see? God gave me specific instructions, but, through my partial lack of faith, what I thought was a good thing –staying at Pillar of Hope – has now made Pillar of Hope and the Peculiar People enemies. Just like Issac and Ishmel. You know Issac was a huge part of the Christian faith. And, on the other hand, Ishmel is a significant part of the Muslim faith," said Brenden.

Natalie was speechless; she didn't know what to say. "Brenden, you thought what you were doing was right."

"Yes, but doing the work of the Lord, a simple mistake can…" Brenden trailed off as he put his head down.

He looked at Natalie and said, "Come, let me show you something."

—

Adams and Sharron had a small chance to enjoy each other's company. With the rigorous planning of Adams choosing the people he wanted in his joint cabinet, and Sharron still consulting until the middle of January, it had been hard to spend quality time together. But Adams penciled in some uninterrupted time when they could be together.

Adams put his phone down and turned to his wife with a soft smile. "I'm glad we could steal a little time for ourselves."

Sharron returned his smile, her eyes reflecting gratitude. "Me too. It feels like we've been ships passing in the night lately."

Adams nodded, a hint of weariness in his expression. "All this planning and decision-making can be exhausting." He huffed frustratedly but paused, "But it's worth it if we can make a difference."

This dreadful prophecy was a curse and a gift. On the one hand, it caused him to depend more heavily on her. But Sharron noticed a change in her husband's mannerisms. Adams had started to get more aggressive, impatient even. So, this dinner was a time to re-engage and relax.

Sharron recognized the slight irritation in her husband's voice. Sharron walked towards him and put her hand on his. "Baby, I know it can be stressful, but hey, you got this. Anyway, enough talk about work. I have fixed your favorites."

She gracefully walked back to the island counter to grab their plates and sat them down, uncovering the tops.

Steamed came up from the hearty meal, like it was fresh out of the oven.

"Mmmm, this smells delicious," he said as his mouth started to water.

His gaze fell onto the plate before him, a masterpiece of culinary art. A succulent chicken breast, perfectly seasoned and roasted to perfection. The vibrant green spears of asparagus danced on the plate, enticing the senses with their aroma. And nestled next to them was a mound of rich and creamy mashed potatoes, filled with the tangy notes of sour cream and the velvety smoothness of buttermilk. Each bite was a symphony of flavors, a perfect harmony of textures that left his tastebuds singing for more.

The President-elect prayed for the food as they said their amens, and then they commenced eating.

"We really haven't had alone time to talk about it, but how are you feeling about going to Alora's for the prep meeting next week?" Sharron asked as she took the first bite of her roasted chicken breast.

Adams hesitated, "I, I don't want to think about it."

He paused as if her question shifted the mood of the room. "My love, you said something at Alora's that I didn't even think about. I'm so used to looking at the cup half full, looking for the good in everything, you know. Believing in God for strength and restoration. I mean, you know me. I don't go to church every day. I may not have the strongest faith, but I do have faith. God is the Father, Jesus Christ is His Son, and the Holy Spirit inhabits the Earth. But you said, what if Alora's can't fix what is wrong with me? And Natalie said, what if my quitting is the starting point of the prophecy?"

He stopped as he shook his head.

Sharron grabbed her husband's hand as he shed tears. "Yes, to answer your question, yes. I think about it every second of every day."

Adams pulled away from the Sharron's touch and bolted up from the table with an overwhelming amount of impatience. "I just don't understand why we have to wait. They, they could do the treatment tomorrow. The planning, precaution, and preparing," he yelled. "I'm just tired of wasting time!"

Sharron got up to comfort her husband. "Honey, I know you are scared. I am—"

"You know what scares me, Sharron? All these people are trying to come up with ways for me to avoid this prophecy. All these plans and schemes. I should step down, or go to Alora's, or let fate be the deciding factor – trust in who I am and what I stand for. But what if, what if no matter what I choose, it ends up being the same outcome, the same atrocious curse? The same unspeakable ending? No matter what direction I go, I can't escape it. I can't hide from it or run away. This prophecy is going to come to pass, regardless; it is inevitable."

A shriek shattered the air. 'Kirk—let me go!' Sharron gasped, her voice raw with fear. Adams blinked, his grip tight on her shoulders. When had he grabbed her? The realization hit him like a punch to the gut. He yanked his hands away, horrified. What had he just done? As soon as Sharron was free, she ran upstairs, crying. Adams reached out to her to say he was sorry, but the window of apology had abruptly closed. Adams had no clue why he had just done that heinous act; furthermore, he had no recollection of doing it. He felt a jolt of fright creeping up his spine and grabbed his suit jacket, knocking over the chair while he moved hastily toward the door.

—

Natalie and Brenden were riding in Natalie's car to a special place he wanted to show her.

Brenden asked, "What do you know about President-elect Adams?"

"He's a good man. He wants the best for America and is willing to fight for the things he loves," Natalie said like she was reading out of a pamphlet.

"That's well and good," Brenden said. "But what do you know about the President?" he asked again comically.

She giggled. "We had a meeting with him, and we told him about the prophecy."

"What did you tell him specifically?"

"I told him about many of my enhanced had dreams of him committing mass murder and genocide."

"So, what did you not tell him?" asked Brenden.

Natalie said hesitantly, "I made it sound like the vision happened, like, a couple of days ago, but they have been happening since you left."

"Nat, come on!" bellowed an irritated Brenden.

Natalie pleaded her case. "Come on Nat, what? I did my due diligence with every three enhanced visions. I did investigations on him and consistently found nothing. Not a shred of evidence, his life is so clean, it's almost unreal."

Brenden sat there, quiet. It was like Natalie's statement took Brenden's fight away.

Natalie asked, "So, in your prophecy, why do you say President Adams is the anti-Christ?"

"Because he is."

Natalie rephrased her question. "No, I guess what I'm asking is, in all the other visions of him, Dimensions saw him as a mass murderer or committing genocide, but you saw him as the anti-Christ. Why is that?"

"Your mind won't go out of the realm of understanding." Brenden paused; his gaze focused on the confusion etched on Natalie's face. "In the Bible, in Revelation, John described visions and dreams of different things he encountered in the future. Most people thought he was speaking in symbols, but what if the things he saw were so far beyond his knowledge that he could only describe them to the best of his ability?"

"Like, if he saw a car, like the one we are in now, when wagons hadn't even been invented yet. Can you imagine trying to explain a car to someone who has never seen one before? The possibilities are endless, but it still has to fit within our understanding and perception. It's like if someone from forty years in the future tried to explain their society to us now."

He took a deep breath before continuing, "I said all of that to say, the enhanced individuals are not knowledgeable about God's Word in an intimate way. They may be seeing glimpses of the anti-Christ, but their understanding is limited by their perception and experiences. Just like how John struggled to explain his visions."

Natalie remembered why she'd fallen head over heels for him.

Beth said, "Your destination has been reached."

Midtown Mall's imposing structure loomed ahead, its dark and empty windows a stark contrast to the lively atmosphere of the past. After an infestation of underground rats, it had been forced to shut down seven years ago. The health inspector discovered tunnels beneath the mall that had been used in 1822 to hide African American slaves. Despite extensive clean-up, the mall struggled to regain popularity due to its dark history with rats.

Brenden had put his mask back on, and Natalie followed his lead. They got out of the car and walked to one of the boarded-up entrances.

"This is the reason why we stopped calling the President-elect the anti-Christ. About six years ago, I started to get real radical with my message, extremely forceful, very deliberate. I noticed I started to get attacks and death threats. I was at the point where I didn't care who I offended. But we started to get major traction, and people started to give us land. I started to think, if somebody killed me, who would continue this holy work? And then I started to think of the long haul, and my message transformed. And I had visions of what could be. And three brothers gave us the deed to all that you see before you," he said as they looked around at the building in the darkness. "I realized the importance of my place in God's plan."

Natalie let out a sarcastic, "Wow, this, this is nice."

With a resounding thud, the Good Shepherd opened an old, rusted keypad and punched in a series of numbers.

The keypad lifted up to reveal a sleek, modern display screen. He placed his pointer finger on the screen, which scanned his fingerprint with a beep. The machine's mechanized voice echoed through the room, saying, "Please ensure all limbs are within the designated square." A bright square of light illuminated around their feet as the floor beneath them began to sink and transform into an elevator. As they descended deeper into the earth, the walls glimmered with advanced technology, and hushed whispers of secrets hidden within these underground tunnels filled the air.

"Oh my God!" Natalie exclaimed as she looked around at the vivacious scenery.

On the main floor, people bustled about in a well-orchestrated symphony of everyday life. They went about their daily tasks with the precision and routine of a well-oiled machine. Housing units lined the periphery of the open space, each one meticulously maintained and uniformly outfitted. In the center, a sprawling atrium extended upward to the second floor, letting in warm, artificial sunlight.

"The architecture here is simply stunning. How long have you all been building this?" asked Natalie.

"We started in early March of 2018. The Bible says, 'And I will restore to you the years that the locust hath eaten and the cankerworm…'" He paused to take in their accomplishments. "Wow, it's only by the act of God that we have massively excelled," said Brenden as he, too, got nostalgic.

The education floor was an oasis of quiet learning amidst the bustling hive of activity. Children sat cross-legged on expansive rugs, their eyes wide with curiosity as they listened to stories of the world.

Natalie and Brenden walked by a lot of children running towards class.

"It's eight o'clock at night; why are the schools still open?" asked a perplexed Natalie.

Brenden puffed his chest out and a sly smirk overwhelmed him. "We are not bound by the weight of time. Also, education is the most important thing, so school runs all day, every day."

The production floor was hidden from the public eye, yet its fruits and vegetables were enjoyed by all. Here, machines whirred and clanged day in and day out to produce food for the inhabitants. Large hydroponic gardens grew vegetables and grains under artificial lights while synthetic proteins were made in a lab nearby. The smell of fresh bread wafted upwards from industrial ovens, creating an olfactory blanket that somehow felt comforting – a stark contrast to the cold metallic surfaces that surrounded it.

Natalie looked at a nice, ripe green apple. "May I?"

Brenden nodded. She took a bite. The apple was crisp and juicy, with a perfect balance of tart and sweet flavors.

Natalie's eyes rolled. "Mmm, this is delicious."

Brenden jokingly said, "Give me a taste," and Natalie very gently hand-fed him the apple.

They once again became captivated with the moment. As Brenden very softly took her hand. Natalie became slightly flustered. She interrupted the giddy feeling.

"What's that machine?"

Brenden responded, "That is our filtration system. It recycles human waste into reusable water.

Natalie grinned at this childlike shyness she was overtaken by.

"Our community is small, but it's growing rapidly. We're currently in the process of constructing two additional floors. We use solar panels and wind turbines down the road, but soon we won't need them. With this new power source we are building, it will allow us to be completely self-sufficient and disconnected from the rest of civilization," said Brenden.

Natalie said, surprised but saddened, "This place is phenomenal, but it's sad that this is all to get ready for the anti-Christ." She hung her head in sorrow.

"If God is still showing me this vision and prompting me to get the followers ready, then the anti-Christ is sure to come."

Natalie let out a pleading, "But to say it is our President, when all the findings pointed at nothing? Looking into his history, he has no past of violence or anything. I even secretly got Judge Mathew's backing towards a warrant for Adams. After two months of carefully surveilling him, we found nothing."

"Do you think that whatever changes him will have to be sudden and psychological?"

"I don't know, but I feel Adams going to Alora's is the perfect way to get in front of it. Instead of letting the madness unleash itself, we have a chance to save him," said Natalie.

Brenden doubled down. "No matter, if God is still preparing me, the anti-Christ is still to come…"

"Well, has the Bible ever stated that God wasn't sure of his choice?" Natalie interrupted with a very inept question.

"God is not like us, He doesn't make mistakes," said Brenden.

Natalie let out a disappointed, "The Bible has to mention at least one time when God wasn't sure about a decision He made."

"No, no… Wait, there was an instance when God changed His mind. It was King Hezekiah, a renowned king of Judah. He holds great significance in the biblical narrative. His story is recounted primarily in Second Kings, Second Chronicles, and Isaiah."

Brenden saw a Bible on one of the tables and opened it as Natalie followed him attentively.

"Hezekiah's reign, lasting from approximately 715 to 686 BC, was filled with religious reforms, political challenges, and a strong reliance on God's guidance. His life and actions teach valuable lessons about faith, leadership, and the power of prayer.

"During his reign, Hezekiah implemented extensive religious reforms. He reopened the temple, repaired its doors, and reinstated the Levitical priesthood. He also called for the celebration of Passover after it had been neglected for many years. This celebration was not limited to Judah – Hezekiah invited the northern kingdom of Israel, recently conquered by Assyria, urging them to return to worshipping Yahweh. These efforts to unite the people in worship showed his commitment to spiritual renewal and national unity," Brenden said, skimming through the books while Natalie looked on, intrigued.

"Toward the end of his life, King Hezekiah fell ill and was told by the prophet Isaiah that he would not recover. In response, Hezekiah prayed to the Lord and reminded Him of his faithful devotion and good deeds. The Lord heard his plea and instructed Isaiah to go back and instruct Hezekiah that he would add fifteen more years to his life as a result of his prayers and tears.

"So, in essence, God made the change after the king's prayer," Brenden said.

Natalie said earnestly, "So, with enough prayer and will, through empathy, God will alter a person's destiny?"

"But that's a very big hope, Natalie. You have to understand there are huge things in play. There are puppet masters working effortlessly in the background, getting ready for the anti-Christ coming."

Natalie said, "It would help if we knew who these people were."

Brenden's stoic gaze was directed toward the elevator, and he let out a concerning, "My leaving Dimensions was not just a vision I received from God, but I was forced out by outside forces as well."

"Do you know their name?" asked Natalie.

"It was Senator Bryan Carter; let's go to my house," said Brenden.

Overture 9 – Conscious and Subconscious

Some theologians say that the very first iteration of our consciousness came when Adam and Eve ate of the tree of good and evil. Their perception shifted, their minds leaped far ahead of their spirits, severing their direct connection to God. In exchange, humanity began to rely on physical senses, particularly sight, as our new 'spirit.'

We now trust what we see above all else. But reality extends beyond the senses, just like love, faith, and forgiveness, which exist without being physically detected.

The subconscious is tricky because it is the unconscious power of the mind. Meaning that the subconscious engages in different stimuli, without your consciousness perception, so to speak. Have you ever heard practice makes perfect or something becoming second nature? That is when you practice a skill so much, it becomes ingrained in you.

That is exactly when something leaves your consciousness and enters your subconsciousness. But all of that filters into the soul.

How amazingly constructed we are!!

Marcus Douglas

Chapter 9 – Playing with People's Souls

Natalie and Brenden had made it to his house.

Natalie picked up the papers Brenden had given her, the series of articles of all the information that Prophet McDowell had gathered on Senator Carter over his seven-year span.

When Carter aggressively prompted Brenden to step down due to his visions of President Adams, Brenden was going to present these documents of his many atrocities at the 2017 Congressional Hearing for Homeland Security on February second. But the information Brenden found had made him afraid.

"Yes, this is the information they need to see," let out an excited Natalie.

Prophet McDowell said, "No, I can't use that."

"So, I'm lost. If you have evidence that could get Senator Carter off the playing field, why not use it?"

"Nat, it's not that simple. There are things in my life that have changed. Things that would be detrimental if I lost."

"What's more important than returning to Dimensions and taking your life back?" Natalie tried to sway him.

"Please, Natalie, have a seat."

He ushered her to the chair in his living room. Natalie sat down, confused, but gave Brenden her undivided attention.

"Nothing fueled me more than taking down Senator Carter and stepping back into my position. As you will see from those documents, I found dirt on Carter. Unconstitutional and illegal dealings. I had direct dates. I had witnesses who were willing to testify. I had enough dirt on him that would bring him up on multiple counts of fraud, espionage, theft, and other charges," Brenden said.

He sat on the couch right in front of Natalie.

"God gave me a dream. I was in a courtroom, following the case of the State vs. Carter. Everybody was heavily watching the case. The judge said, 'Is there a verdict?' The bailiff got the paper from the juror, and he handed it to the judge. The judge said, 'All rise,' and then he read off all the charges. It was all nine charges that I submitted on the senator, and he was found not guilty. The Carter legal team was elated. Everybody started to stand, and they had these faintly seen strings coming from the back of their necks. And every string to every connected person all went to the senator's hand. Carter slowly looked back at me and smiled."

Brenden grabbed Natalie by the hands and said, "I kept having dreams similar to that one. But I kept going, insisting I would bring the senator down. The day before the session with Congress, a very good friend I trusted wanted me to meet him at his house. I showed up later that night, and he invited me into his living room. And there was the Speaker of the House, a lot of high-ranking Democratic and Republican officials, and the Vice President.

"They were all there to get me to recant my findings on Senator Carter. They were all speaking so recklessly about him. Some of them knew what he had done and still defended him. I saw firsthand the level of control the senator commanded. I asked, 'Why are you all doing this? Do y'all not see what he stands for?' Then Senator Carter was standing by the door with that same devilish smile he had taunted me with in my dreams. I ran out the door, terrified, not sure if I was going to make it home."

Natalie bellowed, "We can stop him! Did you ever think it might be his decisions that will bring the President to this heinous prophe—"

"Natalie…?" Brenden interrupted.

"No, no, Brenden, I will not believe we are defenseless. Dimensions can stop this. I know it!"

"Natalie, please," Brenden said as he got up from the seat, emotional. "You know, you sound just like me. Headstrong, determined, full steam ahead, but with all the mistakes I have made. The truth is, my nonbelief caused me to create these two factions that will soon be at war with one another. God keeps giving me the way to go, and I go another way. But look at all the people who are caught in the fallout. This is about life and death, and I'm so cavalier with playing with people's souls. But now I know what I must do."

Natalie got up and gently took Brenden's hand. "Listen, I have pull within the government. I can get you an audience, and we…"

Brenden once again saw the engagement ring on the necklace around her neck and interrupted her. "Natalie, why are you really here? Are you trying to get to the bottom of why I stepped down? Are you trying to understand this prophecy I got nine years ago? Are you just checking up on an old friend?" he asked as he responded to her touch by switching the placement of his hands on hers to a more intimate setting.

Natalie's words stumbled out of her mouth, anxiety tightening its grip on her. Nervousness coursed through her veins, and the fluttering of butterflies in her stomach was as evident now as it had been a decade ago. It felt as though Brenden possessed some secret knowledge about her true self, effortlessly dismantling the facade she had crafted over the years. Like butter melting under the oppressive heat of a summer's day, all her defenses melted away in his presence.

Natalie battled against her own desires. The need to reach out and wrap her arms around him threatened to consume her, but she fought against it with every fiber of her being. Yet, as the battle waged on, a sense of sanctification washed over her, compelling her to surrender to the yearning in her heart.

Natalie felt a surge of warmth as Brenden's face gently touched her shoulder, sending shivers down her spine. It was as if her entire body was enveloped in a chill, caught between the desire to resist and the pull of their connection. They swayed to a lovely melody that played only in their minds, a symphony of love and longing. Or perhaps it was a battle for supremacy, an unspoken struggle between their hearts and the boundaries set by their respective roles.

Brenden knew all too well the lines he shouldn't cross. His position demanded restraint and adherence to higher principles. Natalie, on the other hand, longed for simplicity and was really hesitant to complicate it further. The question lingered in the air like a delicate whisper: Who would give in first?

As Natalie's mind wandered back eight years ago, memories flooded her thoughts like a rushing river. She found herself transported to another time, another place where the threads of destiny intertwined.

September 7, 2016

Natalie was at a fancy restaurant in Virginia called A Piece of Heaven. She waited with excitement as the luxurious ambiance enveloped her. Her outfit was enchanting – a wine-colored, low-neck gown with a side split, revealing her slender figure. A dazzling choker adorned her neckline, while diamond earrings dangled from her ears. Her meticulously crafted hair was elegantly styled into a bun, held in place by chopsticks. In one hand, she held a white purse adorned with cubic zirconia.

No more than seconds after, a figure emerged through the entrance. Brenden exuded a sense of refinement and elegance as he confidently strode in his smoke-gray three-piece suit. The wine-colored velvet accents on the suit demanded attention and respect. To complete his unique style, he wore matching wine-colored velvet shoes that added a touch of sophistication to every step. His wrist was adorned with a sparkling watch and bracelet set, mesmerizing all who caught a glimpse. And his slicked-back hair gave off a hint of villainy, reminiscent of iconic gangster movies.

Brenden walked up on Natalie and kissed her. "Hello, love, I'm sorry I'm late. Traffic was an absolute nightmare," he said as he lightly touched her shoulders while sitting down across from her.

Natalie responded with a smile that could light up a thousand moons. "That's quite all right, dear." Her eyes danced as she took him in, appreciating the man standing before her. She often dreamed that she would be in this exact position with the man of her dreams.

As Natalie gazed at Brenden, she felt a soft warmth spreading through her body, akin to the feeling of being wrapped in a cozy blanket on a cold winter's night. She could almost feel his thumb softly tracing circles on her hand, creating a gentle tingle that sent shivers down her spine. His words were like a caress against her skin, filling her with a sense of comfort and belonging. It was as if he had reached out and laid his heart in her hands, and she couldn't help but be touched by the depth of his love for her.

Brenden said, "Natalie, I loved you from the moment I laid eyes on you, and I fell for your beauty as well as your character.

"So many times, I longed for a woman of your elegance, your grace, and your innocence."

Natalie's eyes sparkled with anticipation and tears of happiness.

Brenden got down on one knee as Natalie put her hand over her mouth.

"Natalie Sofia Massey, will you marry me?" he asked as he presented a beautiful engagement ring with diamonds that shined so brightly. It displayed a very distinct sequence.

Natalie let out a very emotional, "Yes!"

Brenden stood up and put the ring on Natalie's finger as they hugged and kissed.

Present Day

Their eyes were fixed on one another, and then Natalie put her head down in shame. She started to think about all the mistakes she had made. The innocent girl she was, was a forsaken dream. A total contrast from the woman who stood before him. Natalie thought she didn't deserve this love. She shook her head and withdrew from Brenden completely. Natalie's fingers tightened around the papers. Her breath came shallow. She swallowed hard, trying to suppress the emotions clawing their way to the surface. "I… I think I should go," she whispered.

Brenden was confused. She still had the engagement ring he given her over eight years ago. The fact that she was there, whatever the reason, was a clear indication that part of her wanted to see him.

Brenden stepped closer to Natalie as she stood up from retrieving the papers. She turned, and he was right in front of her. Brenden slowly put his hand toward her neck to reveal the necklace with the engagement ring. He hung his head to hide his emotion. Brenden let out a heartbroken question that seemingly siphoned all the air out of the room. "Nat, where did we go wrong?"

Natalie started to speed walk toward her jacket, hopeful that avoidance would keep her protected from the questions.

"Why won't you answer me? At least look at me?" he asked as he quickly followed her around the room.

Natalie felt an overwhelming of discomfort and slight pit of fear, Natalie blurted out, "Beth, can you bring the car around front?"

The car circled around the front porch as the doors opened.

Brenden pleaded with her but then asked a question that would stop Natalie in her tracks. Natalie put her hands on the door of the car to get in, and Brenden asked simply, "Natalie, do you still love me?

With all her heart, she wanted to answer yes. But something held her back, something that withdrew her from the very fairytale ending she always dreamed of.

Natalie fixed her mouth to say, "It's not… I will… I never should have come here. I'm sorry…"

"I'm ready!" she said as the suicide doors closed.

Brenden stood and stayed glaring at Natalie as the car drove away.

And thirty-minutes later, Natalie sat in the car, in front of her hotel, still reeling from everything that had happened.

Natalie finally went inside and commenced drowning in sorrow. Her heart longed for nothing like a relationship with the love of her life. Even now, his presence was like an enticing aroma she couldn't break free from. Yes, going to revisit him had been a terrible idea. But her focus couldn't be on Brenden, it had to be on the President-elect and the mission. She slowly pitted her gaze on the documents from Brenden's house.

Natalie looked over the first document, and it didn't read like a document revealing Senator Carter's atrocities. It read like a memoir.

—

August 23rd, 2007: Democratic Debate.

"Welcome to the third Democratic debate. I'm your host, Eric Bradshaw. If you are all in our prestigious crowd at the esteemed Completion Center Building in the illustrious Charleston, South Carolina, we thank you for your presence. If you are a part of the millions watching at home on television, we applaud you. Now, for our two candidates, on the right of me is the diligent senator, Jacob Payne, and on the left of me the uncompromising senator, Bryan W. Carter. Gentlemen, please keep in mind that there are five minutes on the timer for each answer. Alright, let's begin.

"My first question is urgent and pressing. We have failed to act in the face of genocide before, as we did in Rwanda in 1994. Now, once again, our nation has a chance to prevent it from happening, but will we take action? What will you, as our President, put into place?"

Jacob's voice rose as he spoke, his eyes blazing with urgency. "We cannot continue to turn a blind eye to the ongoing genocide in Africa. We failed in Rwanda, and we are failing now. As President, I will implement a no-fly zone and impose economic sanctions, leveraging our relationships with European countries and even China to put an end to this crisis. And let us not forget about the rampant rape and violence that plagues these nations – we must find ways to stop it."

Carter interrupted, his tone stern and forceful. "A no-fly zone is not enough. We need a protective force on the ground as well. But more importantly, we need to address the root issues in Africa before they escalate into crises." As he finished speaking, Carter's voice echoed with determination and resolve to make a real change in Africa.

Jacob responded, "Oh, Senator, please! You say a no-fly zone is not enough, but it is a start and very cost-efficient compared to all the other ideas!"

"Senator, I'm not saying we shouldn't explore that option. I'm saying we need to do more. This means looking beyond immediate solutions and investing in trade opportunities, economic development, and stable foreign policies for these nations. Our long-term security depends on providing equal opportunities for children in Sudan, Zimbabwe, Kenya, and all of Africa so they have a chance at a better future instead of succumbing to violence and chaos," said a determined Carter.

It went back and forth with Carter's statements being more prevailing and resonating. With this presidential race on both sides, it seemed like not only was Senator Carter ahead in the Democratic rankings but would also be favored against his Republican adversary as well. However, one event would change his life.

Senator Carter came out of the third debate with a slew of confidence. As he talked among the surrounding people, his assistant approached him with some urgent news.

Senator Carter's assistant grabbed his arm. "Excuse me, excuse me, Senator, your wife has just collapsed!"

Carter said, "Oh no, Lenora!"

He rushed backstage and saw his wife of eighteen years laid out on a stretcher, breathing in an oxygen mask.

The senator grabbed her hand gently and looked at the medical staff and asked what was wrong.

Dr. Zanaya said, "We can't put a finger on what caused her lack of oxygen, but we're about to transport her to Franklin Memorial two blocks down the street for a better assessment."

His mind trialed back seven months prior, after Lenora's MRI results. The senator sat anxiously in the medical facility waiting room, his thoughts consumed by worry for Lenora. Suddenly, a doctor in a white coat emerged from behind the swinging double doors and approached him.

"Mr. Senator, I'm Dr. Turner. I wanted to speak with you about Lenora's condition," the doctor said, his voice calm but serious. "What is Mrs. Carter's profession?"

"She's a highly respected professor at Rock Hill College in Washington, D.C., known for her expertise in Swahili literature and linguistics. Why?"

"I'm sorry, Senator, just trying to get an idea on the cause and the treatment," said Dr. Turner

Carter stood up, his heart racing. "Okay, now you are scaring me. Please, tell me what's going on. Is she going to be okay?" he asked, his voice barely above a whisper.

Dr. Turner cast a gloomy expression. "I'm afraid Lenora has been diagnosed with a rare neurological disorder called idiopathic intracranial hypertension. It's causing increased pressure within her skull due to excess spinal fluid," he explained gently.

The senator felt a wave of fear wash over him as he tried to process the grim news. "What are her treatment options? How can we help her?" he asked, desperation creeping into his voice.

Dr. Turner placed a reassuring hand on the senator's shoulder. "We're exploring different treatment plans, including medication and possible surgical interventions to alleviate the pressure on her brain. See, Senator, there are different things that could be the root cause: tension, stress, or strain. So, the most obvious treatment is a lot of rest. Lenora needs to come off instructing just for a little while," he said, offering some hope with his words.

But, despite the promises of pharmaceutical treatment to slow down the progression of this cruel disease, their hopes were also intertwined with prayers, fighting an unseen battle within Lenora's mind. This dark cloud hovered over all thoughts and conversations, seeming to wash away memories on a swift current beyond reach.

These were the things Senator Carter dwelled on as he stood by Lenora's side in the hospital room, grappling with the weight of her illness and the decision looming over his political career. A gentle knock on the door signaled the arrival of a familiar face.

It was his longtime friend and campaign manager, Thomas Mecklenburg, who entered with a grave expression etched on his face. "Senator," Thomas began, his voice heavy with concern, "I know this is a difficult time, but we need to talk about your next steps in the campaign."

Carter turned to face Thomas, his eyes reflecting a mixture of exhaustion and determination. "I can't believe I have to make this decision now," he murmured, his voice strained with emotion. "How can I continue running for President when my wife needs me now more than ever?"

Thomas placed a reassuring hand on Carter's shoulder, offering a sense of solidarity in the midst of uncertainty. "I understand your predicament," he replied softly, "but the country needs a leader like you. Someone who values integrity and compassion above all else. Your decision will impact not just your family, but millions of Americans looking for hope and stability."

Carter nodded thoughtfully, his mind torn between duty and devotion. He whimpered as he stared at his Lenora with all manner of machines beeping. "I know the American people need me, my voice, my character, my undying commitment. I can usher in a new era of stability and take the United States into a golden age.

"However, if I can't be there for my wife in her time of need, if I can't be trusted with those simple vows, in sickness or in health—" Carter very gently put his hand on her face "—then what kind of man am I? My vows to the love of my life trumps the American people! Thomas, I am going to bow out gracefully. The people may want me, but my wife needs me."

Thomas got up and put his fingertips on Carter's shoulder. It was the unspoken words between the two. The transferal of Thomas' understanding and Carter's commitment and dedication to Lenora spoke volumes through their gestures. The senator gave his wife his total attention as Thomas walked out the door.

Natalie felt a sense of overwhelming sadness while flipping the pages. How could the senator have this ultimate prize and sacrifice it for his loved one? She skimmed through a couple of pages, and she saw Lenora's condition worsened and immediately was compelled to read further.

—

June 22, 2011

Bryan Carter was no longer the senator for Indiana. His pride and joy were taking care of his wife. Though her health was rapidly declining, and she was struggling heavily with her memory, Bryan's faith through God kept him strong. He had no doubts that God would bring his wife out of this turmoil. Bryan was Lenora's life of stability.

The Carters had several investments, three prominent restaurant chains, Manchester's, Hog Dog, and Mean

Cuisine. Their biggest investment was a delivery service called Flamazon; their slogan was getting things delivered with the hottest record times. The Carters purchased the stock when Flamazon was still finding their foot in the market about nine years ago. But now it was an eight-hundred-billion-dollar-a-year business and growing.

Bryan began to understand how deeply in love with his wife he was. Lenora struggled with making short-term or long-term memories. At the beginning, her good days overrode her bad, but now her good days were less frequent. But she remembered everything about Swahili linguistics, so sometimes, she would speak in the Swahili dialect. Bryan started to learn Swahili just so he could have some type of communication with Lenora.

Overture 10 – The Mind

Your mind plays a very dire part in the construction of the soul. I truly believe that when Adam and Eve ate of the tree, it thrust their soul beyond their spirit. It explains why they saw themselves as naked. Because the sin brought vanity to the light. That is why we struggle with believing things of the spiritual world. Have you ever heard the classic saying, 'Seeing is believing'? Our sight became the very sense that we believe in far more than the others. But the Bible says faith comes by hearing and not seeing. So, every day, we battle for our soul, killing our flesh daily to become more Christ-like.

Do you feel like anything is above the power of the mind?

Marcus Douglas

Chapter 10 – Girth of Her Soul

In Alora's, Dr. Eve was meeting with her chosen two Ubuntu Joiners.

Dr. Eve said, "Ladies, thank you for coming. Please have a seat."

"No problem, Doctor." June's bubbly attitude was infectious. "Anything I can do to help, I'm available."

"It is always an honor, Doctor," Passion said as they all sat down.

"So, this case, F7P9, is case of extreme importance. This one patient can usher our company into sunset. This patient can give us the positive exposure that we most desperately need," said Dr. Eve solemnly.

Passion felt unworthy. She knew it was her actions that sent the Demario Evans case to ruins. The question she asked in her soul was, *Why me?*

"Yes! I've been waiting to get on one of the very big cases; thank you for choosing me," said June, as the excitement bubbling inside her.

Dr. Eve said, "Yes, each one of you have been the backbone to this company."

Dr. Eve cried, "And I'm very, very thankful. Alora's would not be half of the company it is today without either one of you. Through the good times and the bad, through our triumphs and our mistakes, we still stand together."

Passion put her head down in grief. "So, the rumors are true?"

"Wait, I'm missing something. What rumors?" asked a perplexed June.

Dr. Eve had a million things she could have said, but the words in her heart went mute. All she could do was nod her head.

"F7P9 is Dr. Eve's final onboarding; then she is retiring," said Passion.

A determined June said, "No, no, Dr. Eve, you can't quit; we need you!"

Passion began to let her core cry out, "When I failed at one of the biggest cases in Alora's history, I came back a shell of myself. I couldn't focus. I was emotionally drained and psychologically torn. All I could think of was how I could do anybody any good in the state I was in? When I was thinking about quitting, I stopped showing up for work. I even contemplated suicide. But, Dr. Eve, I don't know what possessed you to come to my house…"

Passion grew emotional. "When I, I saw you, I, all I could do was hug you and cry. That one day was the beginning of my transformation. It let me know that I needed to face my problems. But it also reminded me I wasn't alone."

"Thank you, Passion and June; you don't know how much your words mean to me. But I'm tired; my soul has reached its final stages. I've sacrificed so much of my being; it's just not the same since, well, since…" said Dr. Eve.

June said, "It looks like your mind is made up, so if you are going to go out, go out on top!"

"Passion?" asked Dr. Eve.

"It's going to be really heartbreaking watching you leave. But I can't expect anybody to stay when their heart is not in it. Just be sure, is all."

———

Natalie continued to read the memoir.

It had been nearly two years since Bryan first began his desperate search for a cure, scouring every corner of the medical world to find something, anything, that could give his wife a chance at a normal life. Although he had complete faith in God, he most certainly put in the work.

He sold some of their stocks and poured all their savings into experimental treatments and medications, each one with its own promising claims and letdowns. But this was the last attempt, the final hope, and after this, there would be nothing left. Bryan felt like he was fighting an impossible battle for his beloved wife's well-being, but the more he fought, the more it seemed like the well was running dry. Money, time, and options were all dwindling away, leaving him with no choice but to pray that this final attempt would bring the relief they both so desperately needed.

It was four p.m., and Bryan was on the computer looking at what stocks he could sell to purchase this new medicine from China. Lenora came to the front of the door with a nurse assisted named Ametrius Hall.

"Jambo, bwana, how are you doing," asked Lenora with makeup on her face.

Bryan was surprised by Lenora's awareness. She was a state higher than what she had been. "Sijambo, how are you doing?"

He looked at her and said as he got up to meet her at the door, "Oh my goodness, you look stunning!"

Lenora started to blush. "Oh, love, thank you. Now, remember, you said on my good days, you would take me out for a night on the town?"

Bryan grabbed her hands ever-so-gently. "I'm willing to go with you to the moon and back. I have an idea – let's get snazzy. We can go to our favorite restaurant."

"Only if you wear that suit I like?" Lenora let out a sly grin and, with a playful but sensual demeanor, softly touched his chest.

Bryan swooped in for a kiss. "I wouldn't have it any other way."

As Lenora walked off to the bedroom, Ametrius said, "She's been doing really good today. What have you been giving her?"

"All of her normal meds, but I did add some burdock root to her vitamins," said Bryan.

Ametrius responded with an approval, "Well, it's most certainly working. Do you need anything from me?"

"No, ma'am, thank you; goodbye Ametrius."

"Goodbye, I'll see you tomorrow."

When Bryan walked Ametrius out the door, he gave his wife a sweet and endearing call, "Lenoraaa, *Lenoraaa.*" But as he walked upstairs in the room, he saw Lenora's feet in the open doorway, shaking.

He went immediately to her aid. "Oh God, Lenora!"

He frantically took out his cell phone and called 911.

—

Bryan sat uncomfortably on the plastic chair in the Baptist hospital emergency room, his foot tapping anxiously against the floor. His mind raced back to the events of just two hours ago, the terrifying moment when Lenora had collapsed on the floor and started shaking uncontrollably. The memory of her trembling body in his arms sent shivers down his spine. He could still hear the echoes of his panicked voice on the phone with the 911 dispatcher, desperately pleading for help as tears streamed down his face. Every second felt like an eternity as he waited for any news about her condition.

Dr. Murphy, the evening emergency doctor, carefully walked up to Bryan. He was sitting down, horrified by his thoughts, his head hanging in the palm of his hand. The doctor sat in the seat right beside him.

Dr. Murphy said, "Mr. Carter, Lenora is stable."

The stress and emotion in Bryan eyes was replaced by relief. An exhale signified a sense of comfort.

Bryan said, "Thank Jesus, I'm so glad that she…"

The doctor shook his head, which interrupted Bryan, to say there was bad news. "Your wife's idiopathic intracranial hypertension has increased significantly. Have your ever heard of Grand Mal seizures, Mr. Carter?"

"No, sir, I haven't," said Bryan.

"The technical name for it is tonic-clonic seizure, a type of seizure that causes loss of consciousness and violent muscle spasms. This is the image that often comes to mind when people think about seizures. During a seizure, there is an abnormal surge of electric activity in the brain, resulting in changes in behavior and movements," explained Dr. Murphy.

Bryan put his head back in his hands, quietly sobbing.

"It gets worse. These seizures can cause an array of health issues, like limbs being paralyzed, extremely painful migraines, excruciating body pain. The brain is a powerful entity – the seizure can trick the brain with a cataclysmic range of electrical signals. Organ failure when there are no physical signs of such a thing. That deceptive communication can eventually lead to strokes and most notably death," explained Dr. Murphy.

As the doctor spoke of Lenora's illness, Bryan couldn't help but break down emotionally. He whispered, "So, are you telling me that, my—my wife's last breath could be at any moment?"

"God forbid. But these attacks are in the beginning stages. Eventually, they will get worse. So, if Lenora's transition comes, I don't want you to be blindsided, Mr. Carter," said Dr. Murphy.

With watery green eyes, Bryan looked at the doctor. And with this terrible news on the horizon, the thought of Lenora's death shattered Bryan's soul into a million pieces. He had always shown strength in the midst of the storm. Bryan's perseverance was always set on Lenora's recovery, but his mind was wrapping around the idea that there might be no light at the end of this tunnel. It was apparent that, at this moment, Bryan slowly started to lose his faith in God. Bryan stammered, as he had a million questions to ask, but he only could let out one. "Umm, is it alright? Can I see her?"

Dr. Murphy said, "She is resting, but yes, you can see her."

—

Natalie's tears fell on the paper as she continued to read. This couldn't be the same man, could it? Carter was a maniacal, power-hungry human being. This version of the senator was none of these things. She turned a few pages and skimmed until she reached a part that said, "Alternative Dreamscape."

August 4th, 2012

Lenora's existence was fading. In the infant stages, she had this will to fight for her life, but now, fear entered every part of her being. Afraid to hope, afraid to believe. The fear of losing both new and old memories. She had forgotten so much in the past few years.

Early one morning, the Carters were just waking up. Bryan's timer had gone off. He let out his morning yawn and turned over to Lenora. "Good morning."

Lenora sat up on the side of the bed, her hands shaking, discombobulated. Her mind was a blur. Not only did she find it hard to focus, but her vocabulary was also depleted. At this point in her illness, she could barely speak. All she could do was stare aimlessly at her quivering hands.

It took Bryan a few seconds to realize what was going on with his wife. But he then saw the shaking and jumped up and went to their bathroom to get her medicines. With much urgency, he grabbed her morning dose and a cup of water out of the bathroom.

"Here you go, sweetie, take these meds," Bryan said as he bent down on one knee to hand-feed her.

As she was taking the medicine, she saw her husband and knocked the meds out of his hand, frantic.

"You are, are not, you, can't, my husband!" she yelled out in the girth of her soul.

Bryan bellowed in frustration, "What are you doing? You need to take these meds!"

But she tried to escape from him in true terror. Lenora attempted to crawl to the other side of the bed towards the door, but her body was so depleted that she fell as soon as she got up. But still, she pulled herself towards the door.

In the descent of Bryan's thoughts, his second greatest fear had moved its way to the forefront. She had forgotten who he was.

Lenora screamed, "Mlagha! Mlagha!"

Which, in Swahili, meant imposter.

Bryan yelled, "Dholuo!"

He got on his knees beside her and said again, "Dholuo."

Husband.

It was like that one word calmed her down. Lenora turned slowly from her stomach onto her back. "Br… Bryan."

"Yes, it's me." He was so relieved that she remembered who he was, but, in the same sentiment, the fact that she had forgotten tore his heart to shreds.

Lenora sat up and gave her husband a hug in solace and comfort. Bryan began to cry. It was like that one instance opened his eyes. Lenora wasn't getting better but worsened by every God-given day. His faith started to erode and wither.

Bryan thought his wife would have been knocking on the door of recovery, but ever since that dreadful diagnosis six years ago, her life had taken a series of pitfalls in a downward spiral.

But the most crucial part was not hearing her voice. The simple things like "I love you" or "thank you" went a long way. At this point, there were a lot of regrets.

He got his wife back into bed and gave her the medicine. Lenora felt horrible, having realized the awful mistake she had made. She kept trying to apologize but couldn't get the words out. Lenora cried as her heart tried to force out the words.

"Umm, be, I, I'm…" she said cryptically.

Bryan cried as well. "Shhh, shhh, it's alright," he said as he kissed her forehead.

Lenora tugged at his pajamas to pull him close, but it was just more broken words.

The doorbell rang. It was Ametrius, the nurse. As Bryan came down to meet her, she hung her jacket in the living room closet.

"Good morning, Mr. Carter, how are we doing today?" asked Ametrius

But Bryan couldn't respond; his emotions had dominated every facet of his body. All he could do was point upstairs. It was like his words stalled, but his gestures were prudent.

Ametrius had never seen Mr. Carter like that. Her pace quickened as she hurried up the steps.

Bryan slumped on the couch, his hands trembling as he fought back tears. His phone buzzed beside him. It was his good friend Thomas.

"Hey, bud, how are you doing?" asked Thomas.

Bryan let out an emotional, "I, I don't think I can do this anymore. My wife's body is breaking down. This morning, she didn't even remember who I was. My own wife feared me. She was frantic. She tried to *escape*."

"Wait, she what?"

Bryan let out a hollow, "Why is God not coming to our aid? I don't understand. He healed my mother and father from cancer and heart disease. I believed He would heal my wife. Her descent in her illness has gradually gotten worse.

"Now Lenora can't even—even speak. And, Thomas, I don't know what else to do. You know what the scariest thing is? The Bible says, in the last days, we will recognize each other by our spirits. But the fact I have completely lost my faith in God, and now my spirit is unrecognizable by my own wife."

Thomas took a deep breath. "Bryan, you always felt like God was going to heal Lenora, but what if that was never

His plan? Hear me out – life and death are a part of living. We all want the best for one another, but that might not always be a person's destiny. Some things can change for the better, but, Bryan, some things are intended to happen just like they are supposed to. It's not right or wrong, it's simply liv—"

"Wait, are you saying—? That this was always God's plan for Lenora to be here in this moment?" Bryan interrupted Thomas frustratedly.

Thomas let out an earnest, "God changes the order of what would typically happen, so, no, sir. Think of His love like a protective blanket in the cold. Now, do you still have to deal with the freezing temperatures? Yes. But now you have a means to make it a little further. This illness is brought about by simply living. What if the illness was supposed to start when Lenora was sixteen and not thirty-eight? What if everything that is going on with her was supposed to be abrupt, but God gave you time? We need to be sure to hold on to the little things that God has given us. And our steadfastness, faith, and character will be the difference maker."

Thomas heard his good friend sobbing on the phone.

"Speaking of which," Thomas said, "I may have something for you all. I've been doing some research, and

I found this place called Alternate Dreamscape. They claim to heal through dreams. It sounded like hogwash, but the company has gotten approved by the FDA for a medicinal drug from Africa. The place is located in San Diego."

Bryan let out a broken, "Could you, uhh, do you think you can get more information on the place?"

—

In the midst of Natalie reading the story about the senator, she slowly drifted off to sleep. And she had a dream that she couldn't tell whether it was real.

The old barn house loomed in the grassy yard, its fading paint revealing ancient wood. The silence was broken by its creaking and the orchestra of crickets and insects. It felt like a horror story, with secrets hidden in every shadow and danger lurking unseen. Natalie stood there, feeling a shiver run down her spine.

Natalie saw an ominous figure standing over three seated, masked gentlemen. They were tied up, beaten, and bruised. The person stood tall, in their black robe and Guy Fawkes mask. They exuded an aura of confidence, but with their ability to be connected to the shadows, they spoke with a distorted voice.

"Do you know who I am?"

The man in the first seat shook his head no frantically. "No, I don't know you or why I am here," he said in sheer terror.

The ominous figure laughed. "Yes, all in due time."

The masked person grabbed the man in the second seat's face and squeezed his chin. Bones cracked in his jaw as he whimpered in pain. The masked person threw the man's head back as he released him.

The man in the second seat said, "Yeah, I know who you are."

The ominous figure snatched off his mask to reveal Prophet Brenden McDowell.

Natalie saw Brenden's face and was in shock. She started to get frantic, knowing she needed to do something, but what? She swiftly looked around, and she saw a lamp in the barn.

"You were the manipulator in the infamous Zachariah Gross case. Operating in the shadows, enhancing every bad quality in a person, and diminishing every good quality. With the wedding ring on your right hand, you are none other than the villainous Lucifer," said the prophet.

A disgusted Lucifer said, "I really do hate that name, but I guess the price of fame comes with unfamiliarity."

"Now, let's reveal the others," said Lucifer.

Lucifer unmasked the man in the first seat. It was President-elect Adams.

"If you know what's good for you, you will release me now!" Adams demanded. "There're many people looking for me."

"Well, Mr. President, they will never find you here," said Lucifer. "And for our last mystery man…"

Lucifer looked out the window, saw a fire burning in the yard, and bellowed, "What's this?"

Lucifer stormed out the door with a Glock 19.

Mere seconds later, Natalie creeped through the back door and said, "Mr. President, let's get you untied."

"Oh, thank heavens, Natalie," whispered a relieved President Adams.

The prophet yelled, "Natalie, you shouldn't be here!"

"I know, I know, but I just couldn't stand around and watch you all die," Natalie said as she walked directly to the second drawer on the dresser and pulled out a letter opener.

As she cut the President-elect's bindings. Everything felt so familiar, but she didn't even think about it.

"Natalie, you are the key to this madness going on with the President. Listen to me quickly. You can break the shackles inside of the President's mind, but you cannot be blinded by greed. You have to be willing to sacrifice everything," said the prophet.

She cut the binds loose, hurried, and moved on to the prophet. He tried to talk fast and keep an eye on Lucifer.

"Natalie, I love you with all my heart. Promise me that you will do the right thing," the prophet said as he started to cry.

"Natalie?" the man from the third seat said, having finally regained consciousness.

Natalie moved in real slow to reveal that third man was Brenden McDowell as well.

"It's you?" asked the prophet convincingly.

"Brenden," Natalie yelled as she looked back and forth.

The prophet said, "That's not Brenden, that's the Good Shepherd. How long were you going to let your secrets and lies catch up to us, huh? Your honesty and your forthcomingness could have prevented all of this."

"Hurry up, Lucifer is coming back," the President-elect said as he looked out the front door.

The Good Shepherd said, "The prophet is honorable, but his information is misconstrued. Everything that is happening with the President being the anti-Christ cannot be stopped. No matter what you throw at it, it can't be prevented."

Natalie said, "But Dimensions…"

"Some things Dimensions holds the power to change, but some things they have no power at all. Dimensions' vision will stagnate. They'll have an array of the different visions, but all about President Adams. But you must not interfere, Natalie, just let the chips fall where they may," said the Good Shepherd as Natalie loosened his restraints.

A frantic President, with a plethora of denial, said, "He has to be lying! We can fix it, Natalie. We can do it. Like the prophet said, you are the key."

"We can't sit back and do nothing. We have to try," pleaded Natalie.

Finally free, the Good Shepherd stood up and said, "No, ma'am, it's going to reach the same rhythmic outcome and dire conclusion if we do something or nothing. This situation is inevitable."

"You are a liar! You're going to lead countless people to death and destruction!" snarled the prophet.

"Death and destruction, huh!? You honestly have no idea, do you? Why are you telling Natalie that she is the key, huh?" The Good Shepherd said as he tried to walk to the prophet, but Natalie held him back. He turned to her and said vigorously, "You are not the savior, Nat, but it's destroyer. If you go into the President's mind, you will be the anti-Christ's accomplice. The only way to soften the blow is never stepping foot in his mind. But it is going to happen."

The prophet said, "But what about hope? Can we just stand by and watch, or do we stand up and fight?"

Lucifer walked back through the front door, and a burst of wind threw Natalie from the house. Everybody used the distraction to flee, but the prophet stood tall and upright. Lucifer pulled up the Glock 19 and pointed it him. The prophet turned and saw Natalie outside in the grass through the window. He mouthed 'I'm sorry' and then was brutally shot five times.

Natalie woke up, frantic and sweating, as her cell phone rang.

She looked at the clock on the wall, and it was 1:12 a.m. She said, "Charles? It's one o'clock in…"

Her secretary interrupted, "I'm sorry, ma'am, but we have an issue of monumental proportions."

"Charles, calm down, what is it?" Natalie's tiredness instantly turned to alertness.

Charles said, "Ma'am, Dimensions is at a cataclysmic halt. I don't really know what's going on."

Charles babbled nervously, "The visions of the Enhanced have been shackled. Everyone is having visions of the President committing genocide."

—

Senator Carter met with Tina Daniels alone in one of his illustrious restaurants at one a.m.

Tina enjoyed every scrumptious bite of her medium-well steak. "This steak is so delicious. Now, I could get used to this."

"This establishment is expecting your bidding; they are anticipating your instructions. Do you want to live like a princess every day? It is all within your grasp, but you have to sacrifice for it," said a convincing senator.

Tina asked, "What is it I need to do?"

"Well, I've been reading the files, and I see you are the lead nurse on F7P9. Congratulations," said Senator Carter.

Tina said, "Thank you. I've worked extremely hard to get this position."

"Tina, you'll be in charge of all the medicines that will be administered. I have a medicine I want you to inject in F7P9." He held it up, mesmerized by its color scheme, but also by its power.

Tina's utensils hit the plate in a state of shock.

"I'm sorry, Senator, but I'm going to have to decline," she said as she got up to leave the restaurant.

"Wait, Tina…"

Tina walked back and asked forcefully, "Do you know what that medicine does? Huh? Cause I do!"

"So, you know of this medicine?" asked a sly senator.

"Dr. Eve spoke of a medicine that Dr. Cudjoe created. It was a highly potent and volatile version of the Zulu. Where did you get this?" asked a nervous Tina.

"What if Alora's wasn't the only establishment that operates in the dream world? Or maybe I got it from somebody close to your Dr. Eve. The VP or LMO for example. The possibilities are endless," said the senator.

"I want no part of it," Tina blurted as she walked toward the entrance.

"Tina, how much debt do you have, hm? You're going through a very costly divorce, and even if you get the house, I don't see you making enough money to keep it. Oh, and I'm sorry to hear about your dad. Dying slowly in America can be extremely expensive."

Tina stopped in her tracks and started to cry, thinking about her dad as she walked back to the table.

"I'm not saying there is no sacrifice, but isn't being financially well off, well, doesn't that supersede the cost?" The senator's words were so convincing.

Tina stood over the senator as he distributed his devilish smirk. She took the small tube of medicine. "You know this medicine will do no harm to the patient, but the Joiners will be the ones with no control."

"Control is not my aim. On the other hand, I want F7P9 to be unleashed," said Senator Carter.

Tina walked out the door.

Carter intertwined his fingers and said confidently, "Checkmate."

Overture 11 – Soul Mate: Part 2

To have a soul mate is to have someone of the opposite sex who is identical to your very being. If the soul of man has all these different aspects working as one unit. A soul mate, in my eyes, must have several roles that are akin to another's life. But, if that is true, then the moniker is, like everything, based on perception. Other than reading about it, how do you know there is a connection that strong? I have never even heard my friends say, "This is my soulmate."

My wife and I have a oneness of the top qualities we hold dear. Not only do we have vast similarities, but we also both strive to build on those characteristics. It is the closest connection I've ever had with the opposite sex.

But we also have characteristics that don't mesh well. My wife has fears I don't have and vice versa. She is a neat freak, and I am not as much. But I love her more because she doesn't view everything as I do. She is who life made her to be.

Is having a soul mate stronger than the concepts of marriage, or are they one in the same?

Marcus Douglas

Chapter 11 – The Tears Her Soul Wanted to Cry

November 22nd, 2024

A yawn enveloped before the typical, "Hello, Natalie?"

Sharron looked at the clock on her dresser. "It's three in the morning. Are you, umm, alright?"

"Hello, Mrs. Adams, I am sorry to bother you. And I know this is going to sound abrupt, but I need to be a part of the team that goes into the President's… head," said a fearful Natalie.

Sharron heard the franticness in her voice and sat straight up in her bed. "Why? What's wrong?"

"Are you near him?" asked Natalie.

Sharron looked at the President snoring, fast asleep. "He's asleep," she whispered.

"Can you go to another room?"

Natalie's request haunted her thoughts, but she remained determined. The room seemed impossible to navigate silently, the box spring creaking with each move. Sharron slid off the bed quietly, careful not to disturb the peaceful breathing of her husband.

Memories of three days ago, when her husband grabbed her shoulders aggressively and shook her violently, clung to her, urging caution as she reached for the door handle with delicate fingers. Despite her gentle touch, a creak betrayed her exit and broke through the stillness.

She froze, her head turning back towards the safety of tangled sheets. There laid the President—unaware and unchanged in his breathing. A wave of relief washed over her before she let out a silent sigh. Stepping into the guestroom, she let out a deep breath, 'Okay."

Natalie said, "The situation has gone from concerning to dire…"

"Oh my God, what could it be?" Sharron said in frustration.

"First Lady, powerful figures – ones with influence over national security – are working against the President. They know about Alora's, and they will sabotage it before it even begins," Natalie said with a plethora of concern.

A baffled Sharron asked, "How did they even know? Our meeting with Alora's was done in secret. They signed a contract specifically for the…" Sharron realized she was raising her voice, then let out softly, "President."

Natalie thought that keeping Sharron in the dark about Senator Carter might be wise, so she played clueless as well. "That's what I've been trying to figure out. Although this person is powerful, they still must be subject to the law. Not unless they are operating outside the law but staying in the shadows and the person who is committing these crimes has not been seen. First Lady, try to make sure you have not been followed."

Sharron whispered, "I'm pretty sure the government has some kind of decoy system."

"There's more. Dimension's dreams and premonitions have stalled. Everybody in my company is having different dreams of your husband becoming this, this mass murderer in different variations. We have to do everything in our power to stop it from happening. This is why I must be on the team that enters the President's mind. You will need someone you can trust in your husband's dreams."

Sharron put her head down. "If the criminal world knew that our most trusted organization is powerless, they would be like kids in a candy store. I will demand that you're a part of the team at Alora's. I will contact them first thing this morning."

"Thank you."

"No, thank you, Natalie," said Sharron as she disconnected the call.

Emotions swirled within the First Lady as she listened to Natalie's strong suggestion, causing tears to well up in her eyes. She reluctantly hung up the phone and brushed away the tears before sneaking back into the room and slipping quietly into bed. Adams stirred slightly, shifting his positions and pulling her close. Sharron flinched at the sudden embrace, still a little off balance from what happened three days ago. Although she longed for his touch, Sharron tried to hold in her tears and give in to the President's embrace.

November 25th, 2024

"Ms. Massey, welcome to Alora's. I hope your flight here was pleasant?" asked Arial.

"Yes, it was. I have a meeting with…"

The clerk interrupted, "With Dr. Eve, yes, ma'am. She will be right down."

Natalie was about to sit down, but Dr. Eve walked through the doors to greet her.

"Ms. Massey, hello, I'm Dr. Ashanti Eve. I've heard so much about you."

Natalie said, "Hello, Dr. Eve, I've heard the same about you after researching this place. I found out we share a lot of the same inner circles."

Eve said, with a Haitian accent, "Natalie, I can't even hide my level of concern when the First Lady demanded you be on the team of Ubuntu Joiners. I immediately denied it. But the First Lady can be extremely persuasive. I looked at Dimensions and started to really research for you and all that your organization has put in place, and it really made me a believer. Not to say I am not skeptic, but let's say I have far fewer reservations."

"Well, it's all about the betterment of President Adams. I'm sure you have a wealth of knowledge concerning dreams. Have you ever seen anything like what the

President-elect is going through?" Natalie asked, feeling like she was rambling senselessly.

Dr. Eve said, "Going in the President's ndoto—I'm sorry, *dreams*, in search of something that hasn't happened yet? No. This will be the first time that we have ever attempted it. We normally change the character of a person after the devastation has been done. That is another reason why having somebody who deals with the prophetic as an Ubuntu Joiner is not such a bad idea. You can maybe see things that we would overlook."

"Well, Doctor, we share equivalence in our practices in a lot of areas. Providing the most comfortable environment for our workers as possible, keeping complete documentation on the ins and outs of the establishment, and being thorough on the legalities – one small misstep could send the whole thing crashing down," said a nervous Natalie.

Dr. Eve said. "Why, yes. However, we make it a point to take care of our Ubuntu Joiner beyond these four walls. As you will see, so many things can affect the therapist. Because of this, it's imperative that they keep their lifestyle clean, and we make sure that they do."

Dr. Eve and Natalie boarded the elevator.

Dr. Eve said, concerned, "Natalie, our first day of assessing in the President-elect's ndoto is December second. We like all our Ubuntu present, so the individual can get comfortable with Joiners who will be inside their head. In essence, we have a week to transform you into a somewhat knowledgeable Ubuntu Joiner. So, there is no right or wrong way for this crash course you are about to receive."

Dr. Eve swiped her keycard on the double doors.

They walked up to one of the recliners, and Dr. Eve directed her hand towards the comfortable seat and said, "Please."

Natalie made her way to the recliner and sat back. The lights in the headrest started to glow. There were two nurse assistants who helped Dr. Eve.

This N.A., Tina Daniels. She is going to assist in this process. Ms. Daniels is going take your vitals, and get the Zulu ready to administer," said Dr. Eve.

Natalie asked, "Zulu?

Tina called out, "One-thirty-two over eighty-seven!"

"The Zulu carries two forms of inner working," Dr. Eve said, "It's derived from ketamine, which enhances brain wave strength so it's easier to make a connection.

Second, it has small traces of ashwagandha, which naturally increases the body's relaxation, making the connection totally comfortable."

Natalie let out a wholesome yawn. "Ashwagandha, ummm, I should have thought of that for relaxation with D.O.A."

"So, Natalie, it's usually about one year before newly trained Ubuntu go into another person's dreams. That aspect of the training is the hardest to get through. Most people struggle to open their mind, to see the connection between the natural world and the dream world. Most people need extensive training, and few people are naturals. But, seeing that you've had dreams and vision dealing with Dimensions, I'm severely hoping that, because of that training, you can traverse the inside of a dream effortlessly," Dr. Eve explained.

As Natalie started to drift, she asked one final question. "How will, how will, I know, know what to look for?"

Dr. Eve turned away and whispered. "You will know it when you see it."

———

Natalie's body plunged from the heavens, a rush of wind whipping through her hair and clothes as she descended towards concrete. The ground seemed to rise to meet her with alarming speed, but just before impact, time slowed to a crawl. It was as if she was cocooned within her own otherworldly bubble, isolated from the world around her. With a graceful landing on her feet, she couldn't help but marvel at the sky that towered above her. A stunning tapestry of shimmering lights and vibrant colors stretched across the beautiful horizon, painting a breathtaking canvas against the midday sky. Shades of electric blues, neon purples, and pulsating pinks illuminated the atmosphere.

As she stood there, raindrops began to drizzle from the heavens above, each droplet carrying a radiant hue that sparkled with an enchanting brilliance. Natalie reached out her hands in awe, hoping to capture one of these magical raindrops within her grasp. Yet, as soon as the droplets touched her skin, they transformed into tiny specks of sparkling light, dissipating into the noon day's air. Though elusive, their beauty lingered in her memory.

Natalie looked up and surveyed the surroundings and then remembered she was there for training. One of the pitfalls Dr. Eve had warned her that the training therapist's minds couldn't separate dream from reality.

She thought again confidently, *I'm in a dream, but in reality, I am here for training.* Then she looked at the houses and each one looked the same. She thought, *How can I tell my house apart?*

Not moments after, a lady appeared and stood behind her and called out to her. "Nat."

Natalie turned, and it was her mother, Rebecca Massey. Natalie was taken aback; she let out a faint, "Mom?"

Rebecca hugged Natalie with tremendous intensity. Natalie tried, with everything in her, to fight the emotions that bubbled up inside. She constantly told herself that this was just a dream, but oh, how her heart wanted to believe this was her actual mother.

"Oh, my little girl, I've missed you so much," said Rebecca as she gave Natalie a second hug. "Aww, what's the matter with you?"

Natalie's heart fought vaguely through the tears her soul wanted to cry. "I can't, I, I can't tell, umm, which house is ours?"

"Because all the houses look alike? Well, the houses may be similar, but there is one thing that separates them, and that's the address. Do you remember our address?"

Natalie slowly turned to the addresses on the mailboxes and said, "I—2847 Brookshire Road."

She was surprised she remembered that exchange with her mother when she was in second grade.

She turned back to her mother, and she was gone. Natalie was right – her mother was not real. But that memory flooded in her heart with an array of emotions. Natalie looked at the mailboxes for the address of her old house. When she found it, the outside looked typical, but the inside was large. She fumbled through the front door and let out the most God-awful cry.

The memory of her mother rested on her soul like a mid-afternoon slumber but resurfaced and met a sea full of tears.

"Mama, I'm sorry. I'm so sorry," she cried out. "I should have never left you behind."

The intensity of her cry increased; her breathing became sporadic. Then she stopped because she heard a sniffle on the far side of the room.

Natalie sat up quickly and yelled, "Who's there?"

"Hello, Natalie, my name is Passion Taylor. I am the Ubuntu Joiner who will be teaching you how to navigate through the dream world," Passion said as she stood up and wiped tears from her eyes.

"By you making it to this point, it means that you're one of a select few. Most potentials don't make it past the entry point. They get captivated in the story that the dream produces. They often forget that they have a goal or purpose, and that's the reason why they're here. The next group can't get past the emotions and memory that the dream has dredged up.

"You undoubtedly made it, but the emotional aspect many students fail at is the graduation test. You have to understand how difficult it is, being in a dream, keeping your emotions in check, and keeping in sight of the goal. And most importantly, you found your nyumba. That's Swahili for house. And yours is quite large and has a lot of totems, which makes it understandable why you are in the one percent," said Passion.

Natalie got up off her knees, looked over, and saw a Guy Fawkes mask and a gun displayed on one of the small tables. Immediately, she got nervous. "I, I have umm, experience with dreams in my profession," she said as she looked frantically around.

"Which is?" asked Passion

"My job?" Natalie asked as she hung her head with her hands above her head, fighting to remember.

"I am the president of D.O.A," blurted Natalie.

Passion nodded. "Follow me." They started walking through Natalie's house, toward her back door.

"So," Passion said, "it is vital that you always remember who you are in reality because that's where we get our instructions from. Whatever changes you need to make to the patient, you have to remember what they are. And if you can't even remember who you are, that means that dreamscape is taking control, and you need to leave here immediately."

Natalie asked, "What happens if you stay in the dream world too long?"

"You start forgetting the real reason you're here, and you start struggling to tell the dreamscape from reality. It's not a grave threat to you personally, but it can be for the patient. Giving them suggestions that are not authorized? What if you tell them to love something that you were sent in to tell them to hate? To draw nearer to something they were supposed to draw away?" said a solemn Passion.

Natalie abruptly let out, "Oh my God, this is, this is beautiful."

They marveled at this bridge-like structure that sat perfectly before them. The Dajara bridge revealed itself in all its splendor. The metallic surface gleamed under the intense rays of the setting sun, casting a warm, golden light across the landscape. Natalie couldn't help but be captivated by its flawless design and vibrant hues that seemed to pulse with energy. Its translucent floor boasting of zero gravity was almost unbelievable. The gentle hum of its grandeur echoed in the distance as she stepped onto the bridge, feeling like she was walking into a heavenly symphony of colors.

"This is the Dajara, the bridge that syncs the patient with the Joiner, putting us on the same neuro pattern. The bridge is harmless. The longer you stay on the bridge, the more we merge, but you don't want to be on the Dajara for longer than an hour. You just want it to filter through your mind, to better assist the patient," explained Passion.

Natalie said with hesitation, "I don't know if I can do this. I have classified information and legal obligations that need to remain private."

"I understand, so instead of us walking together, I will go first. That way, it will be you more molding into my mind than me in yours," Passion said with a wave of understanding.

Passion started to walk onto the Dajara and spent about fifteen minutes before stepping off the golden bridge.

As Natalie stepped onto the Dajara, she felt an immediate connection to the bridge. She could sense its power and uncanny strength. With each step, she fought against the process, trying to maintain control over her own mind. The Dajara was designed to put a person in a state of stasis, deliberately slowing down their movements and reactions. But any sudden or fast movement felt like an intense battle, as if every muscle in her body was straining against invisible weights. She could almost hear the grunting and growling of her own efforts as she struggled to maintain her composure on the bridge. It was a mental and physical challenge, akin to lifting heavy weights in a gym. But Natalie was determined to master the Dajara, no matter how much tension and strain it might cause her.

Natalie collapsed once she fully crossed the Dajara. Her muscles and very limbs were depleted.

Passion ran over to Natalie. "My God, woman, I know the process is uncomfortable at first, but you must let the bridge connect us. This will all be for nothing without a connection."

Natalie vaguely muttered, "I know, I know, but like I said, I have governmental secrets that legally only I can know."

"The patient, whoever they may be, will never transverse the bridge. Its towering wall looms in front of them, blocking their view entirely. As therapists, we have the ability to see it, but the patient cannot. They are unable to merge with our memories, only us with them," Passion explained as she helped Natalie up.

Natalie said, "I don't think the process worked. I don't feel any different."

She stood and started to walk slowly up the apple-wooded banister, trying to pull herself up, after the taxing journey across the Dajara. She walked into the open door like she lived there.

"This is not my house," joked Passion.

Natalie said, "Yes, it is. I would recognize that apple-wood banister anywhere."

Then Natalie stood in awe and asked, "How did I know that?"

"The syncing was successful," Passion said. "Now you have total access to my memories, thoughts, and emotions."

Natalie looked into Passion's house, saw a stuffed doll, and picked it up. "Your dad gave you this when you were five. He won it at the Dixie Classic fair in 1993."

"Oh yeah, how did he win it?" Passion asked as she laughed.

Natalie started to laugh as well. "Jeremiah cheated at the ring toss game. He used his own set of weighted rings he had brought along."

Passion laughed heartily. "Yes, that's my dad. Always the clever one."

Natalie breathed in deeply and closed her eyes as Passion's memories dominated her senses. Natalie smiled as she continued to close her eyes to take in the sublime scent. She exclaimed, "I smell popcorn. It's like it's right in front of me."

As the two women continued to share memories and laughter, they moved deeper into Passion's home. Natalie, still clutching the stuffed doll, felt an intense wave of nostalgia. She could vividly remember the scent of cotton candy and popcorn lingering in the air, the joyous screams and laughter of other fair-goers, and the proud smile on Passion's father's face as he presented his daughter with her prize.

Passion led Natalie upstairs into a room filled with books from floor to ceiling. "This is my sanctuary," Passion said, her voice barely above a whisper.

Natalie slowly walked around the room, her fingers gently brushing against the spines of books that ranged from ancient and crumbling to glossy and new. She felt an overwhelming sense of love for these books – love that came not from her own experiences but from Passion's heart.

She found herself drawn to an old leather-bound book on one of the lower shelves. As she picked it up, a cloud of dust puffed out from between its worn pages.

"This one," Natalie said, "this is your favorite."

"Yes," admitted Passion with a half-smile. "*The Odyssey* by Homer. I've read it so many times that I could probably recite it by heart."

As Natalie opened the book, a folded piece of paper fell onto her lap. Picking it up, she unfolded it to find a hand-drawn map with various locations marked and notated in Passion's handwriting.

"This is your dream world map," Natalie observed as she traced her finger over the rough sketch. "When you were twelve, you wanted to go to these places. You started going door to door, asking the neighbors if you could take out their trash for fifty cents. It wasn't until your dad got cancer that your dreams abruptly ended."

She stared impassively at the wall. "Jeremiah had insurance, but it was colon cancer and they caught it too late. Your dad's body started to deteriorate. I'm sorry. I shouldn't be talking about your life like that." Natalie looked up and saw Passion crying.

Passion let out an earnest, "That's quite alright, Natalie – that's why we are here. Through medicine and science, I wanted you to see the gravitation of Dr. Eve and Dr. Cudjoe's work. How we use it, how it transforms the life of the patients. Come on, let's go back downstairs."

Dr. Eve was below as Passion and Natalie walked down the steps.

"Ms. Taylor, Ms. Massey, how are we coming along?" asked Dr. Eve.

"This place is unbelievable," Natalie said excitedly. "Never in my day have I seen the perfect combination of medicine and science coming together so fluidly. What you have here is truly remarkable and ingenious."

Dr. Eve said, "Thank you, Natalie. Coming from someone who deals directly with the paranormal, that is an enormous compliment. Although we are incredibly efficient, we still have pitfalls."

Natalie asked, "What pitfalls?"

"Not too long ago, we ended up getting a big prison contract to rehabilitate their most vile and sadistic criminals. Among those was a young boy whose name was Demario Evans," said Passion.

Dr. Eve explained, "Ms. Massey, we are in Ms. Taylor's house. Which, in reality, is a direct replica of her human body. That's why, when you synced, you were able to share her memories, her emotions. You were even able to connect to her senses. But if we start to make changes in her house in the dream world, then it will affect her in reality as well. With every significant decision, your mind links it with a totem. Now, in reality, that is not dire, but in the dream world, it is very important. Because these objects can cause instant changes dealing with a person's character, actions, or decisions."

"When you came into my house," Passion said, "you saw the stuffed animal my dad won for me. If I had a terrible relationship with my dad and it started to cause a series of cataclysmic failures, if we made suggestions, or even hid the totems, or changed any item directly connected to my father in the dream world, the memory would alter, and it would be like my father's actions didn't exist in reality. And that would change my character dramatically."

Dr. Eve said, "So, when we went in to start on Mr. Evans, we noticed his nyumba…"

Natalie interrupted, "That means house, right?"

"Yes, Ms. Massey, you got it. So, his nyumba was a mansion. An immaculate construct, we were in awe. We consistently sent Ubuntu in his dreams so the two could be amazed. We decided to use Mr. Evans as our quote-unquote poster boy. We had been in talks with China and India to start chapters in their countries. And it began to work out. Mr. Evans had a lot of trauma – a slew of negative emotions – that we altered or hid," said Dr. Eve.

Natalie hung her head, not in sadness but because she started to remember. She glimpsed into Passion's memories like they were own.

Passion said in sorrow, "I thought I scanned every room in his nyumba before sending him out as a changed man. He became a beacon of hope. He not only radiated light for the people at Alora's, but he developed into a positive figure in the prison system as well.

"But his hatred for his parents, he hid it somewhere I couldn't find. He vowed from when he was seventeen, until he became thirty-six, that he would kill his parents. And February second at 7:49 p.m., he did just that."

Passion started to cry. "When I saw the news, my heart dropped."

Natalie started to cry as well. The feelings weren't her own, but still being highly tethered to Passion's emotions, she felt them all the same. Natalie spoke in so much sadness, "You were, you were thinking about quitting – you even contemplated suicide. It didn't only damage your heart but left your soul in ruins. You viewed Mario like a son. It was hard for you to be his Ubuntu and not be vested in him."

Dr. Eve said, "Natalie, that's why we always have to be aware. The President-elect might want the changes now but might change his tune once you all start. Come on, let's head back."

Overture 12 – Faith

Faith ends the final conversation we have about the soul. Let me break it down. There are two types of faith, the one that you believe in and the one that you believe with.

The Bible says in Hebrews: "Let us hold fast the profession of *our* faith without wavering; for he *is* faithful that promised." That is the faith we believe in, God the Father, Jesus Christ the Son, and the Holy Spirit. But the coin is double-sided. Not only does the Bible state that we should put our full faith in God, but it also gives a reason, because He is faithful that promised.

The second faith is what you believe with. The Bible says also in Hebrews: "But without faith it is impossible to please Him: for he that cometh to God must believe that He is, and that He is a rewarder of them that diligently seek him." This is your faith you carry everywhere you go. But this faith is only strengthened by exercising it. Praying, fasting, reading to get an understanding. Believing in God with pure faith that He will do exactly what He said. And so, with faith, it empowers the soul.

Is God faithful, and that's why He promises, or does He promise, and that's why He is faithful?

Marcus Douglas

Chapter 12 – She Fell in Love with a Fading Soul

December 2nd, 2024

"F7P9 has arrived," the secretary said into their earpieces.

Dr. Eve said simply, "We are ready to receive F7P9."

Although Dr. Eve seemed calm, seeing that this was her last case, Alora's was still her heart. Time and time again, she wondered what she was going to do afterwards. But knowing that she was quitting had put her at peace. As if a massive weight lifted off her shoulders, Dr. Eve even had a start-of-mission celebration. It was where they focused on the details of the case. They shared their dreams of success concerning F7P9 and the things that they would like to see. In that meeting, Dr. Eve discussed the magnitude of success that was riding on this particular mission.

Her team initiated the protocols they'd practiced time and time again. The room was filled with an energy that couldn't be described – anticipation and fear blended into one intoxicating cocktail.

The doors slid open, and in Sharron wheeled F7P9 in a white medical gown. Underneath the cold, metallic exterior lay the President. His face was pale, lips parted and eyes wide open, his mannerisms full of anxious energy. He breathed shallowly – his heart was jittery, but his soul, his soul was prepared.

Since the revelation of this diabolical prophecy and learning about Alora's, he had been nervous but ready, even though this was just a prep meeting to see the kind of operation he needed.

Sharron absolutely wanted this to be a success, even more now than when they both got a whiff of the heinous prophecy. Conversations of the past flooded her thoughts. "Baby, what if they can't fix what is wrong? Honey, I know you are scared…" But now she was scared that the soul of the man who she fell in love with was fading, like that of an unstructured memory. The First Lady arrived at the double doors, where Dr. Eve greeted her.

Dr. Eve said, "Breathe, First Lady, this is just a prep session. We're doing nothing more than going into F7P9's dreams to introduce ourselves and getting him comfortable with his Ubuntu and assessing the kind of care he requires. If everything goes smoothly, it will be a two-hour session, max."

"And if it doesn't?" asked Sharron.

Dr. Eve confidently said, "Then four, but, First Lady, you will have total visual footage on the entire meeting in real time. Then you will have your own personal Ubuntu that will walk you through step by step of our findings."

A gentleman walked up behind Dr. Eve and said, "It's an honor to meet you, First Lady,"

"This is Isaiah Moses," said Dr. Eve, "the Ubuntu Joiner who is going to walk you through the discoveries and the process."

Isaiah said, "Would you follow me, please?"

Seconds later, the Ubuntu Joiners, June Ling, Passion Taylor, and Natalie Massey were in preparation. They all met in front of the double doors on the second floor.

"Passion, how are you doing? I am so glad to see you." June let out a bubbly squeal as she hugged Passion, then looked at Natalie. "I owe every part of me being at Alora's to the excellent training of this incredible woman."

"Yes, I certainly agree! Passion has a heart of gold, and I can say that firmly after syncing with her," Natalie replied, a warm softness in her eyes that contradicted her otherwise stern exterior. She turned to Passion, extending a firm hand. "I never got a chance to thank you for your week of training me. Your patience and understanding really floored me. I thought I was going to be a nuisance, but you really cared."

Passion's tears took precedence as she bypassed Natalie's handshake and gave her a hug. And then June hugged the both.

So much positivity and appreciation are a perfect way to start this journey we are about to take, thought June.

Dr. Eve came through the double doors to an unexpected, lovely energy. At that particular moment, she was proud of their selected Joiners. "F7P9 is ready, ladies."

The Ubuntu disbanded their pleasantries and proceeded through the double doors.

Tina saw that no one was looking at her and proceeded to administer the ZX20 tube. Sweat glistened from her pores; her throat felt dry. It was as if she was in a million places, trying to do several things. But everybody came into the double doors and caused Tina to slip the vial back in her lab coat.

They moved with a purposeful stride, their feet echoing through the wide space as they navigated the cozy, cushion-like seats. As they looked at the President snug away in a deep slumber, they wondered what mysteries to conquer lay in F7P9's mind.

Passion asked confidently, "What are F7P9's vitals?

"His blood pressure is one-thirty-eight over ninety-two; his heart rate is eighty-three b.p.m.," said Tina. "The Zulu was administered at 8:37 a.m."

As they each lay back in the recliners, the illuminated radiance in the headrest started to glow. The numerous lights in the electric head mounts flickered. The Ubuntu Joiners and Dr. Eve drifted off in the comfortable medical chair as the Zulu was administered.

Tina once again saw that no one was looking at her, and she administered the vial Senator Carter gave to her into the President-elect's machine. Her hands shook; the emptiness in her stomach became overbearing. *This is definitely an act of treason,* she thought.

President Adams woke up quietly in his bed. "Where am I?" he calmly asked. He stood up off the bed and looked around in his empty room, not a totem in sight.

"I'm dreaming," he let out faintly as he walked slowly into the kitchen, where there were also no totems. But then he walked into the living room, where he saw precisely eleven totems.

Adams walked slowly to a glass cup on the small table, half full of liquid. He grabbed it, smelled it, and pulled his nose away quickly.

"Pesticide. It was the dreadful day I drank pesticide, mistaking it for water. My mind collected the memory and brought it... into my dreams?"

Adams' gaze shifted from the spiked liquid to the other ten totems neatly lined up across the room. One by one, he began to search for their significance. Inside the dream world, his emotions were still heightened, his heart pounding as he observed the surreal scene unfolding before him.

Meanwhile, back in the real world, the Ubuntu Joiners were deeply ensnared in F7P9's dream state. Their vitals held steady, reflecting their serene calmness, which was much needed for the task at hand.

Tina's voice was like a deceitful lullaby in the background, soothing yet deceptive. "The vitals are stable. They're now fully synced with F7P9," she announced, her eyes darting between the multiple screens displaying the health parameters of everyone involved. They all landed in the dreamscape, and one by one, they made their way towards the Dajara bridge.

Within F7P9's dreamscape, President Adams slowly approached the second totem. It was a beautifully carved trinket with intricate details that sent his mind spiraling into memories long buried in his subconscious. The totem was an exact wooden replica of his award for the Nobel Peace Prize. Adams started to smile; that day changed the way his life was going. "My third greatest accomplishment," he uttered.

Then he began to get up and frantically look around calling, "Sharron, Sharron!"

He called out her name as if she was in the room with him. And then he saw the totem with the phone number his wife had given him so long ago. He picked it up and happily sighed. "Love at first sight."

The President-elect had realized each totem represented a fragment of his life, an event or person that had left an everlasting impact on him.

Moments later, the President-elect fell to the ground, holding his head. It was weird, but he could feel the sharing of his consciousness with the other Ubuntu. Adams fumbled around, trying to force his way toward the outside of his house and saw three people walking across a beautiful translucent bridge.

Natalie made it across first, fighting through the taxing journey that had never gotten any easier. Dr. Eve next, then Passion, and last but not least, June. They were walking toward each other when they saw F7P9's body hanging lifelessly on the banister of the steps.

"June!" Passion screamed as they all ran up on the President-elect.

He whimpered, "I, I felt you, you all mold within my thoughts. It's like it was a transference of my awareness."

Dr. Eve said, "That's not possible. I…"

The President-elect interrupted, "You, you guys came across those, uhh, bridges, right there."

Natalie looked at them, concerned. "I thought the patient couldn't see the Dajara?"

"They're not supposed to be able to see anything but their house and totems inside it," June said, frightened.

Dr. Eve was slow to answer because her mind was still wrapping around the fact that F7P9 could see the Dajara. What the President-elect was displaying looked God-awfully like those medicines her late husband had created.

At the creation of Alora's, Dr. Eve and Dr. Cudjoe started perfecting the dream walk, trying to understand the right meds and dosage. Dr. Eve was the therapist, and Dr. Cudjoe was the patient. The medicines gave him a vast amount of control. However, they had both been after the same goal and understanding.

June yelled, "Dr. Eve, Passion! I think you want to take a look at this!"

They rushed into his house and saw the totems in a perfect line.

Dr. Eve said, "Something is very wrong." She whispered to herself, "Somebody has been in here."

"They are in a phenomenal line. I have never…" June was taken aback. She couldn't fathom how perfectly arranged they were.

Natalie asked frantically, "What does all this mean?"

Passion said, "Let's split up and check for totems in the other parts of the house."

And they all did just that.

Meanwhile, back at Alora's, the First Lady was watching the footage, her emotions all over the place. She broke out in a sea of tears when the President-elect picked up the totem with her phone number and hinted that it was the greatest decision he ever made. But, when the Ubuntu arrived with a lot of improbabilities, Sharron demanded to Isaiah that they get him out of there. But the President-elect couldn't be awoken until the Ubuntu awoke first. Breaking the connection had to happen on their end, or there was a possibility that the Ubuntu would be stuck in the President-Elect's dreams.

When each one of the Ubuntu came back into the living room, they all said no more totems were found.

Natalie stood at the front door with the most defeated stare. As she gazed off in the distance, her eyes grew teary. And then everybody's eyes watered as, through Adams, they were all connecting emotionally. The ZX20's volatileness connected them as like they were all one.

"Oh, no!" said Dr. Eve frantically.

"The Dajara bridges…" said June.

"They are…" said Passion.

"All gone," said a disappointed Natalie.

All the women ran to the front door, and, just like the patient, they now could not see the Dajara.

A frightened but amazed June asked, "Have you all ever seen anything like this before?"

"Never," Passion let out, petrified.

But it had been at least five years since Dr. Eve had been in the President-elect's dreams.

The President had asked if they had ever met, and she had lied. She'd met him before his Nobel prize – she'd been his first Ubuntu and had made the suggestions during those alterations that they had never met.

Which was why the President-elect didn't remember Dr. Eve. Not her, nor the alteration to change him from what he was, into the man he was now.

Natalie asked, "Are we trapped in here?"

"Where is F7P9?" Dr. Eve bellowed, looking around desperately.

Natalie asked, "How are we going to get out of here with no Dajara?"

"We have a fail-safe," said Dr. Eve, still frantically searching for the President.

"The Zulu will deplete from our bodies," Passion explained to Natalie, joining Dr. Eve, "but that's another eight hours away."

June hung her head, disappointed. "What choice do we have? We might as well make the best of the time. Find the totem that is causing this crazy prophecy and attempt to alter or hide it while we're down here."

Passion said, "That's the thing – it's only eleven totems, and all of them are connected to good memories. In fact, these totems are almost story bookish."

"Like the story wasn't experienced but manufactured." Natalie joined into the conversation.

June gave a deeper look at the totems. "Natalie, you're totally right – it's like these totems were written out and attached to F7P9's memory."

"Let's find the President-elect," said a determined Dr. Eve.

The President-elect stood at his back door. With the Ubuntu, it was where their Dajara bridge normally was. However, the President-elect was staring at a massive brick dome. When the women found him gazing off in the distance, he asked, "What is this?"

June said, "Mr. President, it's just a series of houses."

"No, I see no houses, just a humongous brick dome. In my dreams, I am always in front of this massive structure. I walked and walked, but it has no opening," the President-elect said as he stood in awe and started to step down and put his hands on the rough brick.

Passion, June, and Natalie stepped down and rubbed the rough surface.

"I can feel it, but I can't…" June words tapered off

The ground began to tremble, and the President-elect's voice cut through the chaos. "Everyone get back!"

Dr. Eve swallowed, glancing at the President. If what she feared was true, the ZX20 would give him an insane amount of power at his call. Any construct that had been created would be immediately visible.

As each block rose towards the sky, the brick walls of this small city seemed to magically disintegrate. Hidden beneath this layer of bricks was a bustling metropolis with its own unique rhythm and pulse. The sounds of traffic hummed along with the chatter of people, occasional bursts of laughter or arguments, and wailing sirens in the distance.

Skyscrapers stretched upwards like towering redwoods, their glass exteriors reflecting the celestial light. They were home to countless offices where men in suits engaged in corporate battles behind screens, surrounded by piles of legal documents and expensive fountain pens.

The hustle and bustle never stopped. Glossy cars honked impatiently on busy roads while hurried pedestrians walked by, lost in their own thoughts or glued to their screens. Towering billboards advertised various products and services, adding to the sensory overload.

Nestled among the towering buildings were charming homes painted in vibrant colors, lining cobblestone streets. The inviting smell of freshly baked bread drifted from corner bakeries as parks offered a peaceful escape from the chaotic city life. Children played, and couples strolled hand-in-hand under lush green canopies.

They were all taken aback – the President-elect's city was operating like a true city.

June hinted a smile of nervous excitement and walked to the city from the President-elect's yard and said 'remarkable' as she slowly rubbed her hand across the fluorescent golden glow.

"Amazing," Passion said as her hands, too, sparked from the static electricity.

Adams said, "I always knew something extraordinary was behind that dome."

The President-elect walked toward the fluorescent golden seal and put his fingertips, then his hand, as the sparks bounced around his hand. He looked back and reached out his hand and said, "Walk on this journey with me."

June, the adventurous one, looked back at the other Joiners. "You only live once," she said as she got up and grabbed the President-elect's hand.

They all, one by one, got up and grabbed one another's hand. They all were connected and walked into the globe like a stratosphere, and the force-field acted quite similar to the

Dajara. But now, it wasn't molding just memories or emotions – it was syncing the Dimension of the Soul…

To be continued…

www.ingramcontent.com/pod-product-compliance
Lightning Source LLC
Chambersburg PA
CBHW051339020726
47501CB00007B/2178